Teresa
of
WATLING STREET

ARNOLD BENNETT

Introduction by
SIMON HOUFE

The
Book
Castle

First published 1904
by Chatto and Windus

This edition published
September 1989
by
The Book Castle
12 Church Street, Dunstable
Bedfordshire

© The Book Castle, 1989

ISBN 1 871199 15 8 (paperback)
ISBN 1 871199 10 7 (hardback)

**The cover design incorporates a
specially commissioned painting by
Joan Schneider**

Printed by Antony Rowe, Chippenham

Arnold Bennett

I

The tombstone of Arnold's father Enoch in Chalgrave churchyard.

Trinity Hall Farm, Hockliffe — Arnold Bennett's Bedfordshire home, 1900-1903.

II

Bennett in Bedfordshire

The Background of
Teresa of Watling Street

Teresa of Watling Street is Arnold Bennett's only Bedfordshire novel. Bennett, whose reputation stands on his North country novels associated with the Potteries, was a migrant to Bedfordshire for the three years 1900 to 1903. Circumstances rather than choice had dictated this sudden change of scene for the Staffordshire author with his increasingly metropolitan outlook on life, but it was a change that had important consequences. For the first time he was confronted with rural England, still in its long 19th century agricultural sleep and hardly awakened by modernity. It was also in this short space of time that he was to come face to face with illness and death, the last sad months and the equally sad passing of his father. Writing of a visit to Bennett in Befordshire in 1902, the journalist Wilfred Whitten recorded — "At Hockliffe Bennett was between two worlds, the one he had not quite left and the one he had not quite entered."

Arnold Bennett was a thirty-three year old journalist with some notable successes to his name when he came house hunting in Bedfordshire in late 1899 or early 1900. He was the editor of **Woman**, on the staff of the **Academy** and **Hearth and Home** and had been much acclaimed for his book **A Man From the North**. He had sufficient income to live out of London in a modest way, and enough taste for a country life to enjoy its new experiences, above all he felt the duty of a son to have his elderly parents with him. The Dunstable area provided the one essential ingredient to the plan, a good rail link with London, and that is probably why he chose this part of the country.

By January 1900, Bennett was established in the rather gaunt house on the edge of Hockliffe village, known as Trinity Hall Farm. The house of yellowish brick and slate roof was not terribly prepossessing, but its position was magnificent and commanded views of miles and miles of the Bedfordshire Chilterns. It was also secluded, only reached from the main road by its own drive and that main road was none other than the Watling Street. Bennett recognised at once the historical associations and the geographical glamour of Watling Street, its huge length, its extraordinary construction and the drama of the cities and towns that it bisected like a nerve on its stately progress.

"Just recently," he writes, "I had tracked it diligently on a series of county maps, and discovered that, though only vague fragments of it remained in Kent, Surrey, Shropshire, Cheshire and Yorkshire, it still flourished and abounded exceedingly in my particular neighbourhood as a right line, austere, renowned, indispensible, clothed in its own immortal dust. I could see but patches of it in the twilight, but I was aware that it stretched fifteen miles southeast of me, and un-numbered miles northwest of me, with scarcely a curve to break the splendid inexorable monotony of its career. To me it was a wonderful road — more wonderful than the Great North Road, or the military road from Moscow to Vladivostok. And the most wonderful thing about it was that I lived on it."

As the home of a writer, Trinity Hall Farm was ideal. During his time there he completed **Anna of the Five Towns**, wrote some of the stories that appeared in **Tales of the Five Towns**, **Fame and Fiction** and a host of magazine articles. Ideal for a bachelor author, it was not yet perfect as a family residence and improvements had to be made if Mr and Mrs Bennett and his sister Tertia were to join him there. During the summer of 1900, Bennett was busy preparing the house for them and having protracted negotiations with the owner. Trinity Hall was owned by a Bedfordshire man John James Reynal Adams and the lease was negotiated through A. W. Merry, the Leighton Buzzard surveyor. Bennett was quite prepared to improve the property at his own expense, but insisted that the landlord redecorate with wall-papers of his own choosing. "I am extremely particular about the wall-papers that I have to live with, and only this firm [Essex & Co] sells the artistic patterns that I require." In October, Bennett wrote to a friend — "This house is in a frightful mess with workmen, but I am enjoying myself immensely." The older Bennetts moved into Trinity Hall Farm during the autumn and their son could reflect on his new property with satisfaction.

"Upon an evening in early autumn, I, who had never owned an orchard before, stood in my orchard; behind me were a phalanx of some sixty trees bearing (miraculously, to my simplicity) a fine crop of apples and plums, and a mead of some two acres, my mead, upon which I discerned possibilities of football and cricket; behind these was a double greenhouse containing three hundred pendent bunches of grapes of the dark and aristocratic variety which I thought I had seen in Piccadilly ticketed at four shillings a pound — my grapes; still further behind uprose the chimneys of a country-house, uncompromisingly plain and to some eyes perhaps ugly, but my country house, the lease of which, stamped, was in my pocket."

Bennett's study or writing room was evidently in one of the bays facing southwards. "From this study window," he was writing in April 1901," I can see 8 miles to the West, and about 6 to the East. I can see the steam of North Western expresses 6 miles away on the right and the steam of Midland expresses 4 miles away on the left. I shall never have a study more ideally placed than this — not even by the sea. In my opinion the landscape here is superior to the generality of Surrey; there is more behind it ....."

He had been reading books on local history and geology as is evident from his letters, and his references to the Chilterns as "Bunyan's Delectable Mountains" suggest that he had also read the recently published **Bunyan's Country** by the Revd A. J. Foster, 1901. His Journal indicates how interested he was in the village life of Hockliffe, he copies down pieces of the inhabitants' dialogues that amuse him and he notes down drives taken into the surrounding countryside towards Battlesden. It is not difficult to imagine with what suspicion the Bennetts must have been regarded by the village, a family of northerners with strange accents who were continually coming and going and entertaining mysterious visitors from London. Furthermore Bennett himself was trying to be familiar with the villagers, that close knit community with only a few surnames between them who had occupied the same cottages for a hundred years!

It was perhaps this strange juxtaposition of the newcomers with the old inhabitants that first suggested itself for the novel that became **Teresa of Watling Street**. Bennett was working on the story, to be published in serial form, in the July of 1901, although it was not to appear as a book until its publication by Chatto & Windus in 1904.

Teresa of Watling Street is subtitled 'A Fantasia on Modern Themes'. The book is really detective fiction with a slight glaze of modernity provided by the chief characters and their style of life. Bennett sets his fictional family the Craigs in the remote Queens Farm on the edge of Watling Street, the building and domain being a very accurate picture of Trinity Hall Farm in all but name. The village of Hockliffe is identified in the first chapter of the book and is followed by many descriptions of landmarks and landscape, Dunstable with its long High Street and Sugar Loaf Hotel, the Chalk Cutting and the audible chimes of Houghton Regis church. There are frequent mentions of the Craigs catching trains at Leighton Buzzard and even information that they had once lived at Sewell!

Hockliffe village and the passage of Watling Street through it appear in some detail, the White Hart is mentioned and a further nine public houses, which, at the time, may have been only a slight exaggeration. Into this setting of agricultural tranquility come the exotic Craig family, Raphael Craig the sinister banker, his beautiful daughter Teresa and an unacknowledged daughter Juana, who works for a circus. Their entourage is even more surprising, including as it does a stage Irish servant and a bogus Irish handyman. The private detective, Richard Redgrave, is employed to investigate this curious household and, suspectible man that he is, falls in love with the beautiful Teresa. Bennett obviously relishes the two worlds portrayed of utter seclusion and high finance, the first represented by the slow pace of life in the village, the second by the car owning Craigs who seem to be continually dashing to London and back in electric broughams or smart Décauvilles with lights blazing.

The object of a detective story is to stimulate and enthrall, not to present any deep psychological insights to the reader. **Teresa** is an amusing read, with its moments of suspense and an undeniable period charm, but it would be rash to suggest that any of the characters come over very strongly. For the Bedfordshire reader the most engaging passages are those flashes of local colour that are obviously genuinely observed. The chief of these are provided by the entry of a Hockliffe villager, Mr Puddephatt.

Puddephatt is a character sketch of Arnold Bennett's chief aider and abettor in the village, Arthur J. Willison. Willison came of an old local family and was both tailor and horse dealer at Hockliffe, although in the novel he appears as wine merchant and horse dealer. Willison was a well known local repository for country lore, gossip and scandals and a number of these are recorded in Bennett's Journal. His bright and inquistive nature may have recommended him to Bennett and he soon became an indispensable part of the novelist's life. It is through Willison that Bennett bought a dalmatian dog in November 1900, later he negotiates the sale of a trap to him which costs £80 and he is always calling with fowls or a gun to inculcate into Bennett the true country life. Bennett learns to ride under Willison's tuition and when old Mr Bennett becomes ill and dies on the 17th January 1902 and is buried in Chalgrave, Willison continually runs errands for the bereaved family. Most significant of all, Willison, who only died in 1955, was told by Arnold

Bennett that he was to feature in a novel on Watling Street. In the novel Mr Puddephatt is described as "a large stout man, dressed in faded gray, with a red, cheerful face and an air of unostentatious prosperity." Redgrave's dialogue with Puddephatt is a real piece of Bedfordshire badinage, the villager avoiding direct answers although his "eyes continually hinted at things which his tongue never uttered."

But the most enjoyable parts of the book are still those sudden glimpses of the Bedfordshire countryside ...

"The day was jocund, the landscape smiled: in the forty-acre field below the house a steam-plough, actuated by two enormous engines and a steel hawser, was working at the bidding of a farmer who farmed on principles of his own, and liked to do his ploughing at midsummer. The steam-plough rattled and jarred and jolted like a humorous and high-spirited leviathan; the birds sang merrily above it; the Chiltern Hills stretched away in the far distance, bathed in limitless glad sunshine; and Watling Street ran white, dazzling and serene, down the near slope and up the hill towards Dunstable, curtained in the dust of rural traffic."

In such passages, the essential Bennett seems to come fully alive and his connection with the county seems enduring.

SIMON HOUFE

CONTENTS

TERESA OF WATLING STREET

CHAPTER I

THE BANK

SINCE money is the fount of all modern romantic adventure, the City of London, which holds more money to the square yard than any other place in the world, is the most romantic of cities. This is a profound truth, but people will not recognise it. There is no more prosaic person than your bank clerk, who ladles out romance from nine to four with a copper trowel without knowing it. There is no more prosaic building than your stone-faced banking office, which hums with romance all day, and never guesses what a palace of wonders it is. The truth, however, remains; and some time in the future it will be universally admitted. And if the City, as a whole, is romantic, its banks are doubly and trebly romantic. Nothing is more marvellous than the rapid growth of our banking system, which is twice as great now as it was twenty years ago—and it was great enough then.

7

Such were the reflections of a young man who, on a June morning, stood motionless on the busy pavement opposite the headquarters of the British and Scottish Banking Company, Limited, in King William Street, City. He was a man of. medium size, fair, thick-set, well-dressed, and wearing gold-rimmed spectacles. The casual observer might have taken him for a superior sort of clerk, but the perfect style of his boots, his gloves, and his hat precluded such a possibility; it is in the second-rate finish of his extremities that the superior clerk, often gorgeous in a new frock-coat, betrays himself. This particular young man, the tenor of whose thoughts showed that he possessed imagination—the rarest of all qualities except honesty—had once been a clerk, but he was a clerk no longer.

He looked at his watch; it showed three minutes to twelve o'clock. He waited another minute, and then crossed through the traffic and entered the sober and forbidding portals of the bank. He had never before been inside a City bank, and the animated scene, to which many glass partitions gave an air of mystery, would have bewildered him had he not long since formed the immutable habit of never allowing himself to be bewildered. Ignoring all the bustle which centred round the various cash desks lettered A to F, G to M, and so on, he turned unhesitatingly to an official who stood behind a little counter.

'Sir?' said the official blandly; it was his sole duty to be bland (and firm) to customers and possible customers of an inquiring turn of mind.

'I have an appointment with Mr. Simon Lock,' said the young man.

The official intensified his blandness at the mention of the august name of the chairman of the British and Scottish Banking Company, Limited.

'Mr. Lock is engaged with the Board,' he said.

'I have an appointment with the Board,' said the young man. 'My card'; and he produced the pasteboard of civilisation.

The official read:

MR. RICHARD REDGRAVE, M.A.,

Specialist.

'In that case,' said the official, now a miracle of blandness, 'be good enough to step this way.'

Mr. Richard Redgrave stepped that way, and presently found himself in front of a mahogany door, on which was painted the legend, 'Directors' Parlour'—not 'Board Room,' but 'Directors' Parlour.' The British and Scottish was not an ancient corporation with a century or two of traditions; it was merely a joint-stock company some thirty years of age. But it had prospered exceedingly, and the directors, especially Mr. Simon Lock, liked to seem quaint and old-fashioned in trifles. Such harmless affectations helped to impress customers and to increase business. The official knocked, and entered the parlour with as much solemnity as though he had been entering a mosque or the tomb of Napoleon. Fifty millions of deposits were manœuvred from day to day in that parlour, and the careers of eight hundred clerks depended on words spoken therein. Then Mr. Richard Redgrave was invited to enter. His foot sank into the deep pile of a Persian carpet. The official closed the door. The specialist was alone with three of the directors of the British and Scottish Bank.

'Please take a seat, Redgrave,' said Lord Dolmer, the only one of the trio with whom Richard was personally acquainted, and to whom he owed this introduction. 'We shall not keep you waiting more than a minute or two.'

The other directors did not look up. All three were rapidly signing papers.

Richard occupied a chair upholstered in red leather, next the door, and surveyed the room. It was a large and lofty apartment, simply but massively furnished in mahogany. A table of superb solidity and vast acreage filled the middle space—such a table as only a bank director could comfortably sit at. As Richard gazed at that article of furniture and listened to the busy scratching of pens, he saw, with the prophetic vision characteristic of all men who are born to success, that a crisis in his life was at hand. He had steadily risen throughout his brief life, but he had never before risen so high as a bank parlour, and the parlour of such a bank! His history, though a short one, was curious. He came to London from Westmorland at the age of nineteen as a clerk in the Customs. From the first he regarded his clerkship merely as a means to an end; what end he had yet to ascertain. He paid particular attention to his clothes, joined a large political club, and kept his eyes open. His personal stock-in-trade consisted of a rather distinguished appearance, a quiet, deliberate, and confident voice and manner, an imperturbable good temper which nothing could affect, and a firm belief that he could do anything a little better than the average doer of that thing. He desired a University degree, and by working at night for four years obtained the M.A. of London. He practised a little journalism of the sensational kind, and did fairly well at that, but abandoned it because the profits were not large enough. One Sunday he was cycling down the Portsmouth Road, and had reached an hotel between twenty and thirty miles from London, when he met with his first real chance. A motor-tricycle had unaccountably disappeared from the hotel during luncheon. The landlord and the owner of the tricycle were arguing as to the former's liability. Redgrave listened discreetly, and then went to examine the barn-like coach-house from which the motor-tricycle had been spirited away. Soon the owner, who had instructed the police and bullied the landlord, and was now forced to kick his angry heels till the departure of the afternoon train back to London, joined him in the coach-house. The two began to talk.

'You are Lord Dolmer,' said Redgrave at length.

'How do you know that?' asked the other quickly.

He was a black-haired man of forty, simply dressed, and of quiet demeanour, save of unusual excitement.

'I have seen you at the Constitutional Club, of which I am a member. Did you know that a motor-tricycle disappeared from this same hotel a fortnight ago?'

Lord Dolmer was impressed by the youth's manner.

'No,' he said. 'Is that really so?'

'Yes,' said Redgrave, 'only a fortnight ago. Strange coincidence, isn't it?'

'Who are you? You seem to know something,' said Lord Dolmer.

Redgrave gave his name and added:

'I am an officer in the Customs.'

That sounded well.

'I fancy I could trace your tricycle if you gave me time,' he said.

'I will give you not only time, but money,' the peer replied.

'We will talk about that later,' said Redgrave.

Until that hour Richard had no thought of assuming the rôle of detective or private inquiry agent; but he saw no reason why he should not

assume such a rôle, and with success. He calmly
determined to trace the missing tricycle. By a
stroke of what is called luck, he found it before
Lord Dolmer's train left. Over half of the coach-
house was a loft in the roof. Richard chanced
to see a set of pulleys in the rafters. He climbed
up; the motor-tricycle was concealed in the loft.
The landlord, confronted with it, said that of
course some mischievous loiterers must have hoisted
it into the loft as a practical joke. The explanation
was an obvious one, and Lord Dolmer was obliged
to accept it. But both he and Redgrave had the
gravest suspicions of the landlord, and it may be
mentioned here that the latter is now in prison,
though not for any sin connected with Lord Dolmer's
tricycle.

'What do I owe you? Name your own sum,'
said Lord Dolmer to Redgrave.

'Nothing at all,' Redgrave answered.

He had come to a resolution on the instant.

'Give me some introductions to your friends.
It is the ambition of my life to conduct important
private inquiries, and you must know plenty of
people who stand in need of such a man as I.'

Lord Dolmer was poor—for a lord—and eked
out a bare competence by being a guinea-pig in
the City, a perfectly respectable and industrious
guinea-pig. He agreed to Redgrave's suggestion,
asked him to dinner at his chambers in Half Moon
Street, and became, in fact, friendly with the imperturbable and resourceful young man. Redgrave

obtained several delicate commissions, and the result was such that in six months he abandoned his post in the Customs, and rented a small office in Adelphi Terrace. His acquaintance with Lord Dolmer continued, and when Lord Dolmer, after a lucky day on the Exchange, bought a 5-h.p. motor-car, these two went about the country together. Redgrave was soon able to manage a motor-car like an expert, and foreseeing that motor-cars would certainly acquire a high importance in the world, he cultivated relations with the firm of manufacturers from whom Lord Dolmer had purchased his car. Then came a spell of ill-luck. The demand for a private inquiry agent of exceptional ability (a 'specialist,' as Richard described himself) seemed to die out. Richard had nothing to do, and was on the point of turning his wits in another direction, when he received a note from Lord Dolmer to the effect that Mr. Simon Lock and the directors of the British and Scottish had some business for him if he cared to undertake it.

Hence his advent in King William Street.

'Let me introduce you,' said Lord Dolmer, beckoning Redgrave from his chair near the door, 'to our chairman, Mr. Simon Lock, whose name is doubtless familiar to you, and to my co-director, Sir Charles Custer.'

Redgrave bowed, and the two financiers nodded.

'Take that chair, Mr. Redgrave,' said Simon Lock, indicating a fourth chair at the table.

Simon Lock, a middle-aged man with gray hair, glinting gray eyes, a short moustache, and no beard, was one of the kings of finance. He had the monarchical manner, modified by an occasional gruff pleasantry. The British and Scottish was only one of various undertakings in which he was interested; he was, for example, at the head of a powerful group of Westralian mining companies, but here, as in all the others, he was the undisputed master. When he spoke Lord Dolmer and Sir Charles Custer held their tongues.

'We have sent for you on Lord Dolmer's re-commendation—a very hearty recommendation, I may say,' Simon Lock began. 'He tells us that you have a particular partiality for motor-car cases'—Richard returned Simon Lock's faint smile—'and so you ought to be specially use-ful to us in our dilemma. I will explain the circumstance as simply as possible. Will you make notes?'

'I never write down these details,' said Richard. 'It is safer not to. My memory is quite reliable.'

Simon Lock nodded twice quickly and resumed.

'We have a branch at Kilburn, in the High Street, under the managership of Mr. Raphael Craig. Mr. Craig has been in our service for about twenty years. His age is fifty-five. He is a widower with one daughter. He came to us from an Irish bank. Professionally, we have no fault to find with him; but for many years past he has chosen to live thirty-five miles from London, at a farmhouse between the town of Dunstable and the village of Hockcliffe, in Bedfordshire. Dunstable, you may be aware, is on the old Roman road, Watling Street, which runs to Chester. He used to go up to Bedfordshire only at week-ends, but of late years he has travelled between his country home and London several times a week, often daily. He owns two or three motor-cars, and has once been summoned and convicted for furious driving. It is said that he can come to London by road from Dunstable in sixty minutes. When he stays in London he sleeps over the bank premises in the suite of rooms which we provide for him, as for all our managers.'

'You say you have no fault to find with Mr. Craig professionally,' said Richard. 'He does not, then, in any way neglect his duties?'

'The reverse. He is an admirable servant, and our Kilburn branch is one of the most lucrative of all our branches. Mr. Craig has built up a wonderfully good business for us in that suburb. Let me continue. Last year but one a relative of Mr. Craig's, an uncle or something of that sort, reputed to be crazy, died and left him a hundred thousand pounds, chiefly, one heard, in new silver coins, which the old miser had had a mania for collecting, and kept in his cellars like wine. The strange thing is that Mr. Craig, thus made rich, did not resign his position with us. Now, why should a man of large fortune trouble himself with the cares of a comparatively unimportant bank managership? That aspect of the case has struck us as somewhat suspicious.'

'Highly suspicious,' murmured Sir Charles Custer, M.P., out of his beard.

'You naturally—shall I say?—resent eccentricity in any member of your staff?' said Richard sagaciously.

'We do, Mr. Redgrave. In a bank, eccentricity is not wanted. Further—another strange fact— a month ago the cashier of our Kilburn branch, a mediocre but worthy servant named Featherstone, a man of fifty, whose brains were insufficient to lift him beyond a cashiership, and who, outside our bank, had no chance whatever of getting a livelihood in this hard world, suddenly resigned. He would give no reason for his resignation, nor could Mr. Craig give us any reason for it. In the following week Featherstone committed suicide. No doubt you saw the affair in the papers. The man's books were perfectly straight. He was a bachelor, and had no ties that the police could discover. Such is the brief outline of the case. Have you any questions to ask?'

Redgrave paused. When, from ignorance or any other cause, he had nothing to say, he contrived to produce an excellent effect by remaining silent and peering through his gold-rimmed spectacles. 'Only one,' he said. 'What do you want to know?'

'We don't know what we want to know,' said Simon Lock abruptly. 'We want to know anything and everything. Our suspicions are too vague to be formulated, but, as directors of a great financial undertaking, we are bound to practise precautions. We do not desire to dismiss Mr. Craig without a reason. Such a course would be unfair—and unprofitable.'

'May I define your position thus?' said Redgrave. 'You do not precisely fear, but you perceive the possibility of some scandal, some revelations, which might harm the general reputation of the bank. And therefore you wish to know, first, why Mr. Craig runs about Watling Street so much in a motor-car; second, why, being possessed of a hundred thousand pounds, he still cares to work for you; and third, why this Featherstone killed himself.'

'Just so,' said Simon Lock, pleased.

'Just so,' echoed Sir Charles Custer.

Lord Dolmer gave his protégé a smile of satisfaction.

'I will undertake to assuage your curiosity on these points,' Redgrave said, with that air of serene confidence which came so naturally to him.

'And your fee?' asked Simon Lock.

'If I fail, nothing. If I succeed I shall present my bill in due course.'

'When shall we hear from you?'

'In not less than a month.'

That evening Richard strolled up the Edgware Road to Kilburn, and looked at the exterior of the Kilburn branch of the British and Scottish. It presented no feature in the least extraordinary.

Richard was less interested in the bank than in the road, the magnificent artery which stretches, almost in a straight line, from the Marble Arch to Chester. Truly the Roman builders of that road had a glorious disregard of everything save direction. Up hill and down dale the mighty Watling Street travels, but it never deviates. After sixty years of disuse, it had resumed its old position as a great highway through the magnificence of England. The cyclist and the motorist had rediscovered it, rejuvenating its venerable inns, raising its venerable dust, and generally giving new vitality to the leviathan after its long sleep.

To Richard Redgrave it seemed the avenue of adventure and of success. His imagination devoured the miles between Kilburn and Dunstable, and he saw the solitary farmhouse of Raphael Craig, bank manager, motorist, and inheritor of a hundred thousand pounds in virgin silver coin.

CHAPTER II

THE CIRCUS

A WEEK later—and in the meantime he had been far from idle—Richard Redgrave arrived in Dunstable. It was a warm, sunshiny, sleepy day, such as suited that sleepy town, and showed off its fine old church and fine old houses to perfection. There is no theatre in Dunstable, no concert-hall, and nothing ever excites this staid borough save a Parliamentary election or the biennial visit of Bosco's circus. On the morning of Richard's arrival Dunstable was certainly excited, and the occasion was Bosco, who, with his horses, camels, elephants, lions, bears, acrobats, riders, trapezists, and pavilions, had encamped in a large field to the south of the town. Along the whole of its length Dunstable, which consists chiefly of houses built on either side of Watling Street for a distance of about a mile and a half, was happily perturbed by the appearance of Bosco's gigantic, unrivalled, and indescribable circus, which was announced to give two performances, at two-thirty and at seven-thirty of the clock. And, after all, a circus which travels with two hundred horses (chiefly piebald and cream), and with a single tent capable of holding four thousand people, is perhaps worthy to cause excitement.

Richard determined to patronise Mr. Bosco's entertainment—he thought he might pick up useful information in the crowd—and at two-thirty he paid his shilling and passed up the gorgeous but rickety steps into the pavilion. A brass band was playing at its full power, but above the noise of the trumpets could be heard the voice of the showman—not Bosco himself, but an individual hired for his big voice—saying, 'Step up, ladies and gentlemen. To-day happens to be the thirtieth anniversary of our first visit to this town, and to celebrate the event we shall present to you exactly the same performance as we had the honour of presenting, by special command, to Her Majesty the Queen at Windsor last year. Step up, step up, and see our great spectacle, the Relief of Mafeking! See the talking horse! See Juana, the most beautiful rider in the world! Step up! Children half-price to morning performance only.' The big voice made precisely this speech every day of his life all over England.

The circus was well filled, and the audience enthusiastic. The clowns had an enormous success. As for Richard, he was more interested in Juana, the horsewoman. She was a tall and beautiful girl, apparently of the Spanish type. She rode, in a strictly conventional park riding costume, a superb strawberry-roan mare, which at her command waltzed, circled, caracoled, and did everything except stand on its head. Mare and rider were equally graceful, equally calm and self-contained. It was a charming item in the programme, but somewhat over the heads of the audience, save a few who knew a born rider when they saw one. An elephant was brought in, a young man in Indian costume being perched on its neck. The mare and the elephant went through a number of evolutions together. Finally the mare reared and lodged her forefeet on the elephant's tremendous flank, and so situated the strange pair made an exit which roused the house from apathy to wild enthusiasm. Juana was vociferously recalled. She re-entered on foot, holding her habit up with one hand, a light whip in the other. Richard could not help being struck by the rather cold, sad, disdainful beauty of the girl's face. It seemed wrong that the possessor of such a face should have to go through a series of tricks twice daily for the diversion of a rustic audience.

'That wench is as like Craig's girl as two peas. Richard turned quickly at the remark, which was made by one of two women, who sat behind him industriously talking. The other agreed that there was some likeness between 'Craig's girl' and the lovely Juana, but not a very remarkable one.

Richard left his seat, went out of the pavilion. and walked round the outside of it towards the part where the performers entered the ring. Attached to the pavilion by a covered way was a smaller tent, which was evidently used as a sort of green-room by the performers. Richard could see within, and it happened that he saw Juana chatting with a girl who was very much like Juana, though rather less stately. The young man in Indian costume, who had ridden the elephant, was also of the group. Soon the young man went to another corner of the tent, and the two girls began to talk more rapidly and more earnestly. Lastly, they shook hands and kissed, Juana burst into tears, and her companion ran out of the tent. Richard followed her at a safe distance through the maze of minor tents, vans, poles, and loose horses, to the main road. A small, exquisitely-finished motor-car stood by the footpath; the girl jumped on board, pulled a lever, and was off in a northerly direction through Dunstable up Watling Street.

'Is that the road to Hockliffe?' he asked a policeman.

'Yes, sir.'

'It's Raphael Craig's daughter, I bet,' he said to himself, and for some reason or other smiled a satisfied smile. Then he added, half aloud, 'But who is Juana?'

He went back to see the rest of the performance, and he had scarcely sat down before he had cause to wish that he had remained outside. The famous strawberry-roan mare, formerly ridden by Juana, was making a second appearance as the talking horse, in charge of the young man who had shone before in Indian costume, but who now wore the dress of a riding-master. An attendant was walking along the front benches with a bundle of numbered cards. He offered one to Richard, and Richard thoughtlessly accepted the offer. From that moment the eyes of the entire assemblage were upon him.

'The gentleman,' said the young man in charge of the mare, 'has chosen a card. Now, this wonderful animal will tell you the number of the card, and a lot of other interesting information. I shall put questions to the animal, which will answer "Yes" by nodding its head, and "No" by shaking its head, and will count by stamping its off forefoot on the ground.'

Richard was disgusted at being thus made the centre of a trick, but there was no help for it.

'What is the number of the card drawn by the gentleman?' the young man demanded of the mare.

She stamped her foot ten times on the tan.

'Number ten,' said the young man. 'Is that so, sir?'

It was so. Richard nodded. Loud applause.

'Is the holder of the card a married man?'

The mare shook her head. Laughter.

'He is a bachelor?'

The mare lowered her head. More laughter.

'Will he ever be married?'

The mare lowered her head again. Loud laughter.

'Soon?'

Again the mare signed an affirmative.   Shrieks
of laughter.

'To a pretty girl?'

The mare nodded decisively.

'Will they be blessed with many children?'

The mare kicked out with her hindlegs, and ran
as if horror-struck from the ring, amid roars of
rustic delight. This simple trick and joke, practised
for years and years with all kinds of horses, had
helped as much as anything to make the fortune of
Bosco's circus. It never failed of its effect.

The final 'turn' of the show was the Relief of
Mafeking. Under cover of the noise and smoke
of gunpowder, Richard contrived to make a stealthy
exit ; he was still blushing. As he departed he
caught a last glimpse of Juana, who came into the
ring in the character of a Red Cross nurse on the field
of battle.

That evening at midnight Richard issued forth
from the Old Sugar Loaf Hotel in a motor-car.
Bosco's circus was already leaving the town, and
as the straggling procession of animals and vehicles
wandered up Watling Street under the summer
moon it made a weird and yet attractive spectacle
—such a spectacle as can be seen only on the high-
roads of England. Its next halting-place was
eighteen miles north—a long journey.   The
cavalcade was a hindrance to Richard for he
particularly desired to have Watling Street between Dunstable and Hockliffe to himself that
night. He waited, therefore, until the whole of

Bosco had vanished ahead out of sight. The elephants, four in number, brought up the rear of the procession, and they were under control of the young man whose trick with the strawberry-roan mare had put Richard to the blush. There was no sign of the mare nor of Juana.

Watling Street runs through a deep chalk-cutting immediately to the north of Dunstable, and then along an embankment. This region at the foot of the Chiltern Hills is famous for its chalk, which is got from immense broad pits to the west of the high-road. As Richard's car ran through the cutting—it was electrical, odourless, and almost noiseless—he perceived in front of him the elephant herd standing in the road. A little further on he descried the elephant-keeper, who was engaged in converse with a girl. Leaving his motor-car to take care of itself, Richard climbed transversely up the side of the cutting, and thus approached nearer to the pair. He saw now, in the brilliant white radiance of the moon, that the girl was the same girl who had kissed Juana in the circus tent. She was apparently urging the man to some course of action at which he hesitated. Then the elephant-keeper called aloud to his elephants, and the man and the girl, followed by the elephants, and followed also by Richard, passed through an open gate at the northern end of the cutting, and so crossed a very large uncultivated field. The extremity of the field descended steeply into a huge chalk-pit, perhaps a hundred yards in circumference and sixty feet deep, by means of a rough cart-track. At the end of the cart-track, in the bottom of the pit, was a motor-car. Richard watched the elephant-keeper single out one of the elephants and attach it by ropes to the motor-car. Slowly the ponderous and docile creature dragged the vehicle up the steep cart-track. The girl clapped her hands with joy.

'If she is Craig's daughter——' Richard exclaimed softly, and then stopped.

Silhouetted sharply against the night sky was the figure of Juana on the strawberry-roan. Mare and rider stood motionless at the top of the cart-track, and Richard, from his place of concealment, could see that Juana was gazing fixedly into the chalk-pit. The man with the elephants and the girl with the motor-car had not perceived her, and before they could do so she had ridden off down the field. It was a wonderful apparition, a wonderful scene—the moon, the vast hemisphere of the purple sky, the glittering and immense whiteness of the chalk-pit, the exotic forms of the elephants contrasted with the motor-car, and, lastly, the commanding and statuesque equestrienne on the brow. Richard was quite impressed by the mere beauty and strangeness, as well as by the mystery, of it all. What did it mean? Why should Juana, an expert who would certainly receive a generous salary, be riding at one o'clock a.m., seeing that the principal performers, as Richard knew, usually travelled by train from one town to the next? And why should she have followed these other two—the elephant-keeper and the young girl who so remarkably resembled herself? And having followed them and observed their movements, why should she silently depart, without making known her presence? He had been able to examine Juana's face in the strong moonlight, and again he was moved by its sad, calm, cold dignity. Juana seemed as though, at the age of twenty-five or so—she could not be more—she had suffered all the seventy and seven different sorrows which this world is said to contain, and had emerged from them resolute and still lovely, but with a withered heart. Her face almost frightened Richard.

With infinite deliberation the elephants and the motor-car arrived at the top of the cart-track. The three elephants not engaged in hauling appeared to have formed a prejudice against the motor-car; the fourth, the worker, who had been used to dragging logs of teak in India, accepted his rôle with indifference. He pulled nonchalantly, as if he was pulling a child's go-cart, thus, happily, leaving the keeper free to control the other beasts. At length the cortège—it had all the solemnity of a funeral pageant—passed safely into the field and out of Richard's sight towards the high-road. He heard the spit, spit of the petrol-engine of the motor-car, now able to move of itself on the easy gradient, and simultaneously a startling snort and roar from one of the elephants. It occurred to him to hope that the leviathan had not taken it into his gigantic head to wreck the machine. The notion was amusing, and he laughed when he thought how frail a thing a motor-car would prove before the attack of an elephant's trunk. Then he proceeded duly towards the road, hugging the hedge. Once more he heard the snort and the roar, and then a stern cry of command from the keeper, a little scream from the girl, and an angry squeak from the elephant. The spit, spit of the motor-car at the same moment ceased.

When, after some minutes of scouting, he reached the gate and had a view of the road, he rather expected to see the motor-car lying in fragments in Watling Street, with, possibly, a couple of mangled corpses in the near neighbour-hood, and a self-satisfied elephant dominating the picture. But his horrid premonitions were falsi-fied. The keeper had clearly proved the super-iority of man over the brute creation; he was astride the neck of the obstreperous elephant, and the herd were trampling, with their soft, flabby footfalls, down Watling Street, along the sloping embankment, into the deep, broad valley which separates Dunstable from the belt of villages to the north of it. The lady with the motor-car stood quiescent in the road. She had got safely out of her chalk-pit, and was now waiting for the elephants to disappear before proceeding on her journey. Richard hesitated whether to return and examine the chalk-pit or to keep in touch with the lady. What any creature—especially a woman,

and a young woman—could be doing with a
motor-car in a chalk-pit in the middle of the night
passed his wit to conceive. Nor could he imagine
how any sane driver of a motor-car could take
his car down such a steep slope as that cart-track
with the least hope of getting it up again without the assistance of an elephant, or at least a
team of horses. She must surely have been urged
by the very strongest reasons to descend into the
pit. What were those reasons? He wanted badly
to examine the chalk-pit at once, but he decided
ultimately that it would be better to watch the
lady—'Craig's girl.' The chalk-pit would always
remain where it was, whereas the lady, undoubtedly
an erratic individuality, might be at the other end
of the world by breakfast-time. He crept back
to his own car, found it unharmed in the deep
shadow where he had left it, and mounted.

By this time the elephant herd had accomplished
a good quarter of a mile down the gradual declivity
of the embankment. 'Craig's girl' started her
car and followed gently. It seemed, in the profound silence of the night, that the spit, spit of
her engine must be heard for miles and miles
around. Richard started his own car, and rolled
noiselessly in the traces of his forerunner. The
surface of the road was perfect—for the Bedfordshire County Council takes a proper pride in its
share of this national thoroughfare—and the
vehicles moved with admirable ease, Richard's
being about a couple of hundred yards in the rear.

Just at the top of the embankment is a tiny village appropriately called Chalk Hill, and this village possesses a post pillar-box, a Wesleyan chapel of the size of a cottage, and an inn—the Green Man. As Richard swung past the Green Man a head popped out of one of its windows.

'Anything wrong?' asked a man.

'No,' said Richard, stopping his car and lowering his voice to a whisper, lest the girl in front should hear and turn round. 'Go back to bed,' he added.

'Go to bed yourself,' the man said, apparently angry at this injunction. 'You circus-folk, you've got motor-cars now; as if camels and alligators wasn't enough, you've got motor-cars a-grunting and a-rattling. Three blessed hours you've been a-passing this house, and my wife down with erysipelas.'

Grumbling, the man closed the window. Richard laughed at being identified with the retinue of Bosco's circus. He felt that it was an honour, for in the eyes of the village these circus-folk move always in an atmosphere of glory and splendour and freedom.

He passed on. The girl in front was gradually overtaking the elephants, which were scattered across the width of the road. Suddenly one of them turned—the one ridden by the keeper—and charged furiously back, followed more slowly by the others. Evidently the sound of the spit, spit of the motor-car had renewed the animal's anger.

Perhaps it thought: 'I will end this spit, spit once for all.' Whatever the brute's thoughts, the keeper could not dissuade it from its intentions, though Richard could see him prodding it behind the ear with a goad. The girl, 'Craig's girl,' perceived the danger which she ran, and, after a moment's vacillation, began to wheel round, with the object of flying before this terrible elephantine wrath. But that moment's vacillation was her undoing. Ere she could get the machine headed straight in the opposite direction the elephant was upon her and her car. Richard trembled with apprehension, for the situation was in truth appalling. With a single effort the elephant might easily have pitched both girl and car down the steep side of the embankment, which was protected only by a thin iron rail. Richard stopped his own car and waited. He could do nothing whatever, and he judged that the presence of himself and another car in the dreadful altercation might lead even to further disasters.

The elephant stood over the car, waving his trunk, seemingly undecided how to go about his work of destruction; the keeper on his neck called and coaxed in vain. The girl . . . Richard could see only the girl's back; he was thankful that he could not see her face. The other elephants waited in a semicircle behind. Then, after an interval that was like a hundred years, the leading elephant seized the steering-wheel of the motorcar, and, twisting it off the rod as though it had been made of putty, flung it into the road. That action seemed to appease the brute. He turned quietly away and slouched off; his keeper had now ceased to prod him. The other elephants followed meekly enough. The girl on the motor-car did not stir. The peril was past, but Richard found his foot trembling against the foot-brake of his car—such had been his agitation.

The elephant herd was five hundred yards away before the girl gave the slightest sign of life. Then she slowly dismounted, and waved a hand to the keeper, who had also dismounted from the elephant's neck—a wave of the hand that was evidently intended to convey an assurance that she was unharmed and able to take care of herself. The keeper gave an answering signal, and—wisely, as Richard thought—continued his way up the opposite hill.

Richard pulled over the starting-lever of his car and leisurely approached the girl. She had already seen him, since her own car was more than half turned round, and therefore there could be no object in his attempting any further concealment. He drew up by her side and raised his peaked cap.

'That was a nasty position for you to be in,' he said, with genuine sympathy.

'Oh, those elephants!' she began gaily; 'their trunks are so thick and hairy, you've no idea——'

Then she stopped, and, without the least warning, burst into tears. It was a very natural reaction, and no one could wonder at such an exhibition. Nevertheless, Richard felt excessively awkward; excessively at a loss what to do under the circumstances. He could scarcely take her in his arms and soothe her like a child; yet that was just the thing he wished to do.

'Come, come,' he said, and his spectacles gleamed paternally at her in the moonlight, 'it is all over now.'

She pulled out a microscopic lace handkerchief, wiped her tears, and looked at him.

'Forgive me,' she exclaimed; and then smiling: 'It shan't occur again.'

'You are a brave woman,' he said sincerely, 'a very brave woman.'

'How?' she asked simply. 'I did nothing.'

'Most women would have fainted or screamed, and then there is no knowing what might not have happened.' He added, as she made no remark: 'Can I be of any assistance? Have you far to go? I suppose you must have miscalculated your distances.'

'Why?' she asked, in reference to the last remark.

'Oh, it's so late, that's all.'

'It is,' she said, as though the fact had just struck her. 'Yes, I must have miscalculated my distances. Fortunately, I have only about a mile more. You see the yellow house on the hill towards Hockliffe? That is my destination.'

'You are Miss Craig?' he said inquiringly.

'I am. You belong, then, to these parts?'

'I happen to know the name of the owner of Queen's Farm, that is all,' he admitted cautiously.

'I am much obliged for your sympathy,' she said. 'I shall walk home, and send a horse for the car to-morrow morning.'

'I could tow it behind my car,' he suggested.

'Pardon me, you couldn't,' she said flatly; 'the steering is smashed.'

'I had thought of that,' he replied quietly, as he picked up the small broken wheel out of the road. 'If we tie a rope to either end of your front axle, and join them at the rear of my car, your car would steer itself automatically.'

'So it would,' she said. 'You are resourceful. I will accept your offer.' Then she examined his car with the rapid glance of an expert. 'Well I never!' she murmured.

He looked a question.

'It is a curious coincidence,' she explained, 'but we have recently ordered an electric car precisely like yours, and were expecting it to arrive to-morrow—my father and I, I mean. Yours is one of the Williamson Motor Company's vehicles, is it not?'

Richard bowed.

'There is no coincidence,' he said. 'This car is destined for Mr. Craig. I am bringing it up to Hockliffe. You will remember that Mr. Craig asked that it should be sent by road in charge of a man?'

'A man!' she repeated; and, after a pause: 'You are, perhaps, a partner in the Williamson Company?'

'Not a partner,' he said.

It may be explained here that the aforesaid Williamson Company had supplied Lord Dolmer with his motor-car. Richard had visited their office in order to ascertain if, by chance, Mr. Raphael Craig was a customer of theirs, and had been told that he was, and, further, that there was an electric car then on order for him. It was a matter of but little difficulty for Richard to persuade Williamson's manager to allow him to pose for a few days as an employé of the company, and to take the car up to Hockliffe himself. He foresaw that in the rôle of a motor-car expert he might gain a footing at Craig's house which could not be gained in any other way.

When the two cars had been attached, and the journey—necessarily a slow one—began, a rather desultory conversation sprang up between Richard and Miss Craig, who sat by his side in the leading car.

'You, too, must have miscalculated your distances,' she said suddenly, after they had discussed the remarkable beauty of the moon.

'No,' he said, 'I like travelling at night. I admit that I thought Hockliffe considerably further on. I expected to deliver the car about breakfast-time.'

'You will permit us to offer you a bed?' she

said. 'You will be able to get at least five hours' sleep. We breakfast at seven. It is early, but that is my father's custom.'

He thanked her.

'Take the little road on the right,' she directed him later. 'It leads only to our house. In Ireland we call such a road a boreen.'

It was then that he noted a faint Irish accent in her voice.

Richard brought the two cars to a standstill in front of a green gate. Leaning over the gate was an old man.

'Teresa!' the old man murmured.

She rushed at him and kissed him passionately.

CHAPTER III

CHINK OF COINS

'I AM getting on excellently,' said Richard to himself as he descended from the car; but his self-satisfaction was momentarily checked by the glance flashed at him by the old man—a glance which seemed to penetrate at once to that locked chamber where Richard kept his secret intentions and desires.

He returned the glance modestly, and then wondered whether, after all, Mr. Craig was as old as he looked. The manager of the Kilburn branch of the British and Scottish Bank had white hair, rather long at the back, and a heavy white beard; a pale face with prominent bones, the lower jaw large and protruding, the nose fine and delicate, the black eyes deep-set; the forehead was rather narrow, but the bossy temples gave indication of unusual intellectual force. The face was the face of an old man, yet the eyes were young and fresh. Richard remembered that Simon Lock had stated the manager's age to be fifty-five, and he came to the conclusion that this might be a fact, though any merely casual observer would have put it at sixty-five at least.

'Who is——' Raphael Craig began questioning in tones of singular politeness, with a gesture in the direction of Richard, after he had returned his daughter's salutation.

'This is a gentleman from the Williamson Company, dad,' Teresa explained. 'He has brought the new car. He likes travelling at night, and thought our house was much further on.'

Then she explained the circumstance of the elephant's attack.

'Humph!' exclaimed Raphael Craig.

Richard affected to be occupied solely with the two motor-cars. He judged it best to seem interested in nothing else. He blew out the oil-lamps of the old car, and switched off the electric lights of the new one. Teresa turned instantly to the latter, and began to turn the light off and on. Her father, too, joined in the examination of the car, and both father and daughter appeared to be wholly wrapped up in this new toy. Richard had to explain all the parts. He soon perceived that he had chanced on one of those households where time is of no account. Teresa and Raphael Craig saw nothing extraordinary in thus dawdling over a motor-car at one o'clock in the morning by the light of the moon. After a thorough inspection of the machine Teresa happened to make some remark about three-speed gears, and a discussion was launched in which Richard had to join. A clock within the house chimed two.

'Suppose we have supper, dad?' said Teresa,

as if struck by a novel and rather pleasing idea—
'suppose we have supper. The moon will soon be
setting.'

'And Mr.——' said Raphael.

'Redgrave,' said Richard. 'Richard Redgrave.'

'Will sup with us, I trust,' said Teresa. 'True,
there are seven inns in the village, but the village
is asleep, and a mile off. We must offer Mr. Redgrave a bed, dad.'

'Humph!' exclaimed the old man again.

It was, perhaps, a strange sort of remark, yet
from his lips it sounded entirely correct and friendly.

'I am getting on excellently,' mused Richard
once more.

'Mike!' the girl called. 'Micky!'

A very small, alert man instantly appeared round
the corner of the garden wall, running towards
them. He kept his head bent, so that Richard
could not clearly see his face.

'What is it ye'll be after, miss?' Micky asked.

'Take charge of these cars. Put them in the
shed. Perhaps Mr. Redgrave will be good enough
to assist you with the new one.'

Raphael Craig walked towards the house. In
three minutes, the cars being safely housed in a
shed which formed part of some farm buildings,
Richard and Teresa joined him in the spacious
hall of the abode. Supper was served in the hall,
because, as Teresa said, the hall was the coolest
place in the house. Except an oldish, stout woman,
who went up the stairs while they were at supper,

Richard saw no sign of a domestic servant. Before the meal, which consisted of cold fowl, a pasty, and some more than tolerable claret, was finished, Raphael Craig excused himself, said 'Good-night' abruptly, and retired into one of the rooms on the ground-floor. Richard and Teresa were then left alone. Not a word further had been exchanged between father and daughter as to the daughter's adventures on the road. So far as the old man's attitude implied anything at all, it implied that Teresa's regular custom was to return home at one in the morning after adventures with motor-cars and elephants. Richard thought this lack of curiosity on the part of the old man remarkably curious, especially as Raphael and his daughter were obviously very much attached to each other.

'The circus was amusing this afternoon,' Richard remarked.

The talk had flagged.

'Where was it?' Teresa asked.

'At Dunstable,' said Richard.

'Really!' she said, 'I had not heard!'

This calm and nonchalant lie astounded Richard. She was a beautiful girl—vivacious, fresh, charming. She could not have long passed her twentieth year, and her face seemed made of innocence and lilies. Yet she lied like a veteran deceiver. It was amusing. Richard removed his spectacles, wiped them, and replaced them.

'Yes,' he continued, 'I went to the afternoon performance. The clowns were excellent, and there was a lady rider, named Juana, who was the most perfect horsewoman I have ever seen.'

Not a muscle of that virginal face twitched.

'Indeed!' said Teresa.

'I thought, perhaps, you had been with friends to the evening performance,' Richard said.

'Oh no!' Teresa answered. 'I had had a much longer journey. Of course, as I overtook those absurd elephants in the cutting, I knew that there must be a circus somewhere in the neighbourhood.'

Then there was another lull in the conversation.

'More wine, Mr. Redgrave?' Teresa invited him.

He thanked her and took another glass, and between the sips said:

'I am told this is a great chalk district—there are large chalk-pits, are there not?'

'Yes,' she said, 'you can see them from our windows. Very ugly they look, too!'

'So far, good!' Richard privately reflected.

He had, at any rate, learnt that the Craigs had something to conceal.

The hall clock struck three. Outside it was broad daylight.

'That is a quarter of an hour fast,' said Teresa. 'But perhaps it might be as well to go to bed. You are probably not used to these hours, Mr. Redgrave? I am. Micky! Micky!'

The small, alert man came down the side-passage leading into the hall from the back part of the house.

'This is decidedly a useful sort of servant,' thought Richard, as he looked intently at Mike's wrinkled, humorous face.

The Irishman seemed to be about thirty-five years of age.

'Micky,' said Teresa, 'show Mr. Redgrave to his room—the room over here. Bridget has prepared it; but see that all is in order.'

'That I will, miss,' said Micky, but only after a marked pause.

Richard shook hands with his hostess and ascended the stairs in Micky's wake, and was presently alone in a not very large bedroom, plainly but sufficiently furnished, and with some rather good prints of famous pictures on the walls.

'Without doubt,' he said, as he got into bed. 'I have had a good day and deserve a good night. I must take measures to stop here as long as I can.'

He had scarcely closed his eyes when there was a tap at the door, the discreetest possible tap.

'Well?' he inquired.

'It's myself, sorr,' said the voice of Micky familiarly.

'Come in, then, Mike,' Richard said with equal familiarity.

He already liked Micky; he felt as though he had known Micky for many years.

Richard had drawn both the blind and the curtains, and the room was in darkness; he could only discern the outline of a figure.

'The mistress told me to remind your honour that breakfast was at seven sharp.'

'I was aware of it,' Richard said dryly; 'but I thank your mistress for the reminder.'

'An' begging pardon, sorr, but d'ye know where it is you're sleeping?'

'At present,' said Richard, 'I'm not sleeping anywhere.'

'Ah, sorr! Don't joke. Mr. Featherstone slept in this room, sorr. Did ye know Mr. Featherstone?'

'What!' cried Richard, starting up. 'Do you mean the man that committed suicide?'

'The same, sorr. But speak low, your honour. It's myself that should not have mentioned it.'

'Why not?' Richard asked, subduing his voice.

'The master might not like it.'

'Then why do you tell me?'

'They say it's unlucky to sleep in a room where a suicide slept the last night of his life.'

'Then Mr. Featherstone killed himself the day he left here?'

'Sure he did so. And I thought I'd warn you.'

'Oh, well,' said Richard, 'it's no matter. I dare say it won't affect my repose. Good-night. Thanks.'

'I'd like ye to sleep in another room—I'd like ye to,' urged Mike in a persuasive whisper.

'No, thanks,' said Richard firmly; 'I'm settled now, and will take the risk.'

Micky sighed and departed. As soon as he was gone Richard rose out of bed, pulled the curtains aside, and made a minute examination of the room. But he could discover nothing whatever beyond the customary appurtenances of an ordinary middle-class bedchamber. There was a chest of drawers, of which every drawer was locked. He tried to push the chest away from the wall in order to look behind it, but the thing was so heavy that he could not even move it. He returned to bed. At the same time his ear caught the regular chink of coins, such a sound as might be made by a man monotonously counting money. It continued without interruption. At first Richard imagined it to proceed from under the bed, but he knew that this was impossible. Then he thought it came from the room to the left, then from the room to the right. Chink—chink—chink; the periodic noise had no cessation.

'What coins can they be?' Richard asked himself; and decided that such a full, rich chink could only be made by half-crowns or crowns.

He endeavoured to sleep, but in vain; for the sound continued with an exasperating regularity. Then he seemed uneasily to doze, and woke up with a start; the sound was still going on. The hall clock struck five. He jumped out of bed, washed and dressed himself, and went quietly downstairs. The sound had mysteriously ceased. With a little difficulty he opened the hall door and passed out into the garden.

It was a lovely morning; the birds sang ravishingly, and a gentle breeze stirred the cypress-trees which lined the drive. The house was absolutely plain as regards its exterior—a square, solid, British farmhouse. A meadow that was half orchard separated it from the high-road. Away from the house, on the other side of it, and at the end of a large garden, was a long range of low buildings, in the form of a quadrangle, which had, presumably, once been the farmstead; they presented, now, a decayed and forlorn look. Richard walked past the front of the house, under its shuttered windows, across the garden, towards these farm buildings. As he opened a gate in the garden wall he saw Mike issuing cautiously from one of the sheds.

Simultaneously there was a tremendous crash from the house—an ear-splitting crash, a crash that might have been caused by ten domestic servants dropping ten trays of crockery on a brick floor. But the crash had a metallic ring with it that precluded the idea of a catastrophe in earthenware.

Richard and Micky glanced at each other.

CHAPTER IV

MR. PUDDEPHATT

RICHARD saw that Mike was quite as startled as himself at the sound of that appalling crash within the house. But in a moment the Irish man-of-all-work had recovered his wits.

'Sure,' he said, his eyes twinkling, 'the Day o' Judgment has come along unexpected.'

'What was it?' Richard asked.

'Mrs. Bridget must have pulled the kitchen dresser on the top of her,' said Mike. 'Or it's a procession of cups and saucers down the cellar steps and they missed their footing.'

But, in spite of the man's jocular tone, Richard thought he perceived something serious in Mike's face. It occurred to him that the Irishman had guessed the true cause of the noise, and was trying to hide it from the visitor.

'You're up early in these parts,' said Richard, determined to ignore the crash.

'I'm a bad sleeper, your honour, and when I can't sleep I get up and enjoy the works of Nature —same as your honour.' The man looked as fresh as though he had had a long night's rest. 'Like to see the horses, sorr?' he added.

47

'Certainly,' said Richard, following Mike into the stable, which was at that end of the range of farm buildings nearest the house. A couple of Irish mares occupied the two stalls of the stable, fine animals both, with clean legs and long, straight necks. But Richard knew nothing of horses, and after a few conventional phrases of admiration he passed into the harness-room behind the stable, and so into what had once been a large farm-yard.

'No farming here nowadays,' he said.

'No, sorr,' said Mike, taking off his coat, preparatory to grooming the mares. 'Motor-cars and farming don't go together. It's many a year since a hen clucked on that midden.'

Richard went into several of the sheds. In one he discovered a Panhard car, similar to that belonging to Lord Dolmer. He examined it, saw that it was in order, and then, finding a screw-driver, removed the screw which held the recoil-spring of its principal brake; he put the screw in his pocket. Then he proceeded further, saw the other two cars in another shed, and next door to that shed a large workshop full of Yankee tools and appliances. Here, improving on his original idea, he filed the thread of the screw which he had abstracted, returned to the first shed, and replaced the screw loosely in its hole. At the furthest corner of the erstwhile farmyard was a locked door, the only locked door in the quadrangle. He tried the latch several times, and at last turned away. From the open door of the harness-room Mike was watching him.

'I've been on a voyage of discovery,' he called, rather self-consciously, across the farmyard.

'Did your honour happen to discover America?' Mike answered.

Richard fancied that he could trace a profound irony in the man's tone.

'No,' he laughed back. 'But I think I'll try to discover the village. Which way?'

'Along the boreen, sorr; then up the hill and down the hill, and you'll come to it if you keep going. It's a mile by day and two by night.'

Richard reached the house again precisely at seven o'clock. Teresa was out in the garden gathering flowers. They exchanged the usual chatter about being up early, walks before breakfast, and the freshness of the morning, and then a gong sounded.

'Breakfast,' said Teresa, flying towards the house.

The meal was again served in the hall. Richard wondered at its promptness in this happy-go-lucky household, but when he saw the face of the stern old woman named Bridget he ceased to wonder. Bridget was evidently a continual fount of order and exactitude. Whatever others did or failed to do, she could be relied upon to keep time.

Mr. Raphael Craig came out of the room into which he had vanished six hours earlier. He kissed Teresa, and shook Richard's hand with equal

gravity. In the morning light his massive head
looked positively noble, Richard thought.   The
bank manager had the air of a great poet or a great
scientist. He seemed wrapped up in his own deep
meditations on the universe.

Yet he ate a noticeably healthy breakfast.
Richard counted both the rashers and the eggs
consumed by Raphael Craig.

'How do you go to town, dad?' asked Teresa.
'Remember, to-day is Saturday.'

'I shall go down on the Panhard. You smashed
the other last night, and I don't care to experiment
with our new purchase this morning.'

'No, you wont' go down on the Panhard,' Richard
said to himself; 'I've seen to that.'

'Perhaps I may have the pleasure of taking Mr.
Redgrave with me?' the old man added.

'I shall be delighted,' said Richard.

'Do you object to fast travelling?' asked Mr.
Craig. 'We start in a quarter of an hour, and shall
reach Kilburn before nine-thirty.'

'The faster the better,' Richard agreed.

'If you please, sir, something's gone wrong with
the brake of the Panhard. The thread of one of
the screws is worn.'

The voice was the voice of Micky, whose head
had unceremoniously inserted itself at the front-
door.

A shadow crossed the fine face of Raphael
Craig.

'Something gone wrong?' he questioned severely.

'Sure, your honour. Perhaps the expert gentleman can mend it,' Mike replied.

Again Richard detected a note of irony in the Irishman's voice.

The whole party went out to inspect the Panhard. Richard, in his assumed rôle of expert, naturally took a prominent position. In handling the damaged screw he contrived to drop it accidently down a grid in the stone floor.

'Never mind,' said Raphael Craig, with a sharp gesture of annoyance. 'I will drive to Leighton Buzzard and catch the eight-ten. It is now seven-thirty. Harness Hetty instantly, Mick.'

'That I will, sorr.'

'Let me suggest,' Richard interposed, 'that I take you to Leighton in the new car. I can then explain the working of it to you, and return here, retrieve the screw which I have so clumsily lost, and put the Panhard to rights, and possibly mend the other one.'

'Oh yes, dad,' said Teresa, 'that will be splendid, and I will go with you to Leighton and drive the car back under Mr. Redgrave's instructions.'

In three minutes the new electric car was at the front-door. Mr. Raphael Craig had gone into the house to fetch his bag. He came out with rather a large brown portmanteau, which, from the ease with which he carried it, was apparently empty. The car was in the form of a small wagonette, with room for two at the front. Mr. Craig put down the bag in the after-part of the car, where Teresa was already sitting, and sprang to Richard's side on the box-seat. As he did so the bag slipped, and Richard seized it to prevent it from falling. He was astonished to find it extremely heavy. By exerting all his strength he could scarcely lift it, yet Mr. Craig had carried it with ease. The bank manager must be a Hercules, notwithstanding his years!

The five and a half miles to Leighton Buzzard Station, on the London and North-Western main line, was accomplished in twenty minutes, and Mr. Raphael Craig pronounced himself satisfied with the new car's performance.

'If you don't mind, Mr. Redgrave,' he said, 'you might meet me here with this car at two-forty-five this afternoon—that is, if you can spare the time. Meanwhile, perhaps the Panhard will be mended, and my daughter will entertain you as best she can.'

Mr. Craig seemed to take Richard's affirmative for granted. Stepping off the car, he threw a kiss to Teresa, picked up the bag as though it had been a feather, and disappeared into the station.

'May I drive home?' Teresa asked meekly, and Richard explained the tricks of the mechanism.

Speeding through the country lanes, with this beautiful girl by his side, Richard was conscious of acute happiness. He said to himself that he had never been so happy in the whole of his life. He wished that he could forget the scene in the chalk-pit, the mysterious crash, Teresa's lies, the suicide of Featherstone, and every other suspicious circumstance. He wished he could forget Mr. Simon Lock and his own mission. But he could not forget, and his conscience began to mar his happiness. What was he doing in the household of the Craigs? Was he not a spy? Was he not taking advantage of Teresa's innocent good-nature? Bah! it was his trade to be a spy, for what other term could be employed in describing a private inquiry agent? And as for Teresa's innocence, probably she was not so innocent after all. The entire household was decidedly queer, unusual, disconcerting. It decidedly held a secret, and it was the business of him, Richard Redgrave, specialist, to unearth that secret. Simon Lock was one of the smartest men in England, and his doubts as to the *bôna fides* of Mr. Raphael Craig seemed in a fair way to be soon justified. 'To work, then,' said Richard resolutely.

'Don't you like Micky?' the girl asked, with an enchanting smile.

'Micky is delightful,' said Richard; 'I suppose you have had him for many years. He has the look of an old and tried retainer.'

'Hasn't he!' Teresa concurred; 'but we have had him precisely a fortnight. You know that Watling Street, like all great high-roads, is infested with tramps. Micky was a Watling Street tramp. He came to the house one day to shelter from a bad thunderstorm. He said he was from Limerick, and badly in need of work. I was at school in

a Limerick convent for five years, and I liked his
Irish ways and speech. We happened to be desperately in need of an odd man, and so I persuaded
father to engage him on trial. Micky is on trial
for a month. I do hope he will stop with us. He
doesn't know very much about motor-cars, but we
are teaching him, and he does understand horses
and the garden.'

'Only a fortnight!' was all Richard's response.

'Yes, but it seems years,' said the girl.

'I was much struck by his attractive manner,'
said Richard, 'when he came to my room last night
with your message.'

'My message?'

'Yes, about breakfast.'

'That must be a mistake,' said Teresa. 'I never
sent any message.'

'He said that you desired to remind me that
breakfast was at seven o'clock.'

Teresa laughed.

'Oh!' she said, 'that's just like Micky, just like
Micky.'

The frank, innocent gaiety of that laugh made
Richard forget Teresa's fibs of the previous night.
He could think of nothing but her beauty, her
youth, her present candour. He wished to warn
her. In spite of the obvious foolishness of such a
course, he wished to warn her—against herself.

'Has it ever occurred to you, Miss Craig,' he
said suddenly, and all the time he cursed himself
for saying it, 'that Mr. Craig's—er—mode of life,

and your own, might expose you to the trickeries of scoundrels, or even to the curiosity of the powers that be? Permit me, though our acquaintance is so brief and slight, to warn you against believing that things are what they appear to be.'

There was a pause.

'Mr. Redgrave,' she said slowly, 'do you mean to imply——'

'I mean to imply nothing whatever, Miss Craig.'

'But you must——'

'Listen. I saw you at the circus yesterday, and in the——'

He stopped at the word 'chalk-pit.' He thought that perhaps he had sacrificed himself sufficiently.

'At the circus!' she exclaimed, then blushed as red as the vermilion wheels of the electric car. 'You are an excessively rude man!' she said.

'I admit it, he answered.

'But I forgive you,' she continued, more mildly; 'your intentions are generous.'

'They are,' said Richard, and privately called himself a hundred different sorts of fool.

Why, why had he warned her against espionage? Why had he stultified his own undertaking, the whole purpose of his visit to Queen's Farm, Hockliffe? Was it because of her face? Was Richard Redgrave, then, like other foolish young men in spring? He admitted that it appeared he was.

When they arrived at the farm Richard

deposited his hostess at the front-door, and ran the car round to the outbuildings, calling for Micky. But Micky was not about. He saw the stable-door open, and, dismounting, he entered the stable. There was no sign of Micky. He went into the harness-room and perceived Micky's coat still hanging on its peg. He also perceived something yellow sticking out of the inside pocket of the coat. He made bold to examine the pocket, and found a French book—the Memoirs of Goron, late chief of the Paris police.

'Rather a strange sort of Irish tramp,' Richard thought, 'to be reading a French book, and such a book!'

With the aid of the admirable collection of tools in Mr. Raphael Craig's workshop, Richard, who was decidedly a gifted amateur in the art of engineering, set to work on the damaged motor-cars, and an hour before lunch-time both the Panhard and the Décauville voiturette were fully restored to the use of their natural functions. He might easily have elongated his task, after the manner of some British workmen, so as to make it last over the week-end; but he had other plans, and, besides, he was not quite sure whether he wished to continue the quest which he had undertaken on behalf of Mr. Simon Lock.

At twelve o'clock he made his way to the house, and found Micky weeding the drive. The two mares were capering in the orchard meadow which separated the house from the road.

'Well, Mike,' said Richard, 'I see you've lived in France in your time.'

'Not me, sorr! And what might your honour be after with those words?'

'You weed in the French way,' Richard returned—'on hands and knees instead of stooping.'

It was a wild statement, but it served as well as another.

'I've never been to France but once, your honour, and then I didn't get there, on account of the sea being so unruly. 'Twas a day trip to Boulogne from London, and sure we had everything in the programme except Boulogne. 'Twas a beautiful sight, Boulogne, but not so beautiful as London when we arrived back at night, thanks to the Blessed Virgin.'

'Then you are a French scholar?' said Richard.

'Wee, wee, bong, merci! That's me French, and it's proud I am of it, your honour. I've no other tricks.'

'Haven't you!' thought Richard; and he passed into the house.

Mike proceeded calmly with his weeding. On inquiry for Miss Craig, Bridget, with a look which seemed to say 'Hands off,' informed him that the young lady was in the orchard. He accordingly sought the orchard, and discovered Teresa idly swinging in a hammock that was slung between two apple-trees.

'Well, Mr. Redgrave,' she questioned, 'have you found that lost screw?'

'I have found it,' he said, 'and put both cars in
order. What with three cars and two horses, you
and Mr. Craig should be tolerably well supplied
with the means of locomotion.'

'Yes,' she said. 'After all, the horses are the
best.' She sat up in the hammock and called
'Hetty!' One of the mares lifted its head, whinnied,
and advanced sedately to the hammock. Teresa
stroked the creature's nose. 'Isn't she a beauty,
Mr. Redgrave? See.'

In an instant Teresa had sprung on the mare's
back, and was cantering, bareback and without
bridle, across the meadow. Hetty was evidently
docile to the last degree, and could be guided by
a touch of the hand on the neck.

'What do you think of that, Mr. Redgrave?'
asked the girl proudly when she returned.

Richard paused.

'It is as good as Juana,' he said quietly. 'I had
no idea you were such a performer.'

Teresa flushed as she slipped easily to the
ground.

'I am not such a performer,' she stiffly replied.

'I came to tell you,' said Richard, ignoring her
petulance, 'that I have to go to a place in the
village on some other business for my firm. I
will get my lunch at one of the inns, and be back
at——'

'Now, Mr. Redgrave,' she interrupted him,
'don't be horrid. I have told Bridget to prepare
a charming lunch for us at one-fifteen, and at one-

fifteen it will be ready. You cannot possibly leave me to eat it alone.'

'I can't,' he admitted. 'At one-fifteen I will be here. Thank you for telling Bridget to get something charming.' He raised his hat and departed.

Now, the first dwelling in the village of Hockliffe as you enter it by Watling Street from the south is a small double-fronted house with a small stable at the side thereof. A vast chestnut-tree stands in front of it, and at this point the telegraph wires, which elsewhere run thickly on both sides of the road, are all carried on the left side, so as not to interfere with the chestnut-tree. Over the front-door of the house, which is set back in a tiny garden, is a sign to this effect: 'Puddephatt, Wine Merchant.' Having descried the sign, the observant traveller will probably descry rows of bottles in one of the windows of the house.

As Richard sauntered down the road in search of he knew not what, Mr. Puddephatt happened to be leaning over his railings—a large, stout man, dressed in faded gray, with a red, cheerful face and an air of unostentatious prosperity.

'Morning,' said Puddephatt.

'Morning,' said Richard.

'Fine morning,' said Mr. Puddephatt.

Richard accepted the proposition and agreed that it was a fine morning. Then he slackened speed and stopped in front of Mr. Puddephatt.

'You are Mr. Puddephatt?'

'The same, sir.'

'I suppose you haven't got any Hennessy 1875 in stock?'

'Have I any Hennessy 1875 in stock, sir? Yes, I have, sir. Five-and-six a bottle, and there's no better brandy nowhere.'

'I'm not feeling very well,' said Richard, 'and I always take Hennessy 1875 when I'm queer, and one can't often get it at public-houses.'

'No, you can't, sir.'

'You don't hold a retail licence?' Richard asked.

'No, sir. I can't sell less than a shilling's worth, and that mustn't be drunk on the premises. But I tell you what I can do—I'll give you a drop. Come inside, sir.''

'It's awfully good of you,' said the brazen Richard; and he went inside and had the drop.

In return he gave Mr. Puddephatt an excellent cigar. Then they began to talk.

'I want a lodging for a night or two,' Richard said after a time; and he explained that he had brought a motor-car up to the Queen's Farm, and had other business in the district for his firm.

'I can find ye a lodging,' said Mr. Puddephatt promptly. 'An aunt o' mine at the other end of the village has as nice a little bedroom as ever you seed, and she'll let you have it for a shilling a night, and glad.'

'Could you arrange it for me?'' Richard asked.

'I could, sir,' said Mr. Puddephatt; and then reflectively: 'So you've come up to Queen's Farm with a motor-car. Seems they're always having motor-cars there.'

'I suppose they're perfectly safe, eh?' said Richard.

'Oh, they're safe enough,' Mr. Puddephatt replied emphatically. 'Very nice people, too, but a bit queer.'

'Queer? How?'

Mr. Puddephatt laughed hesitatingly.

'Well,' he said, 'that Miss Craig's knocking about these roads on them motor-cars day and night. Not but what she's a proper young lady.'

'But everyone goes about on motor-cars nowadays,' said Richard.

'Yes,' said Mr. Puddephatt. 'But everyone doesn't pay all their bills in new silver same as the Craigs.'

'They pay for everything in new silver, do they?' said Richard.

'That they do, sir. I sold 'em a couple of Irish mares when they first come to the Queen's Farm. Dashed if I didn't have to take the money away in my dog-cart!'

'But is it not the fact that an uncle of Mr. Craig's died a couple of years ago and left him a large fortune in silver—an old crank, wasn't he?'

'So people say,' said Mr. Puddephatt sharply, as if to intimate that people would say anything.

'It's perfectly good silver, isn't it?' Richard asked.

'Oh, it's good enough!' Mr. Puddephatt admitted in the same tone as he had said, 'Oh, they're safe enough!' a few moments before.

'How long has Mr. Craig lived at the Queen's Farm?'

'About two years,' said Mr. Puddephatt.

Mr. Simon Lock, then, was wrongly informed. Mr. Lock had said that Craig had lived at the farm for many years.

'Where did he come from?'

'Before that he had a small house under Dunstable Downs—rather a lonesome place, near them big chalk-pits,' Mr. Puddephatt answered. 'He seems to like lonesome houses.'

'Near the chalk-pits, eh?' said Richard.

'As you're a motor-car gent,' said Mr. Puddephatt later, 'I reckon I can't sell you a horse.'

'I thought you sold wines and spirits.'

'So I do. I supply the gentry for miles around; but I does a bit in horses—and other things. And there isn't a man as ever I sold a horse to as I can't look in the face this day. I've got the prettiest little bay cob in my stable now——'

Richard was obliged to say that that was not his season for buying horse-flesh, and, thanking Mr. Puddephatt, he left the wineshop.

'A house near the chalk-pits,' he mused. Then he turned back. 'I'll let you know about the room later in the day,' he said to Mr. Puddephatt.

'Right, sir,' answered Mr. Puddephatt.

Richard could not refrain from speculating as to how much Mr. Puddephatt already knew about the Craigs and how much he guessed at. Mr. Puddephatt was certainly a man of weight and a man of caution. The wine-merchant's eyes continually hinted at things which his tongue never uttered.

CHAPTER V

FIRE

THE luncheon with Teresa was a pronounced social success. French rather than Irish in character, it was eaten under a plum-tree in the orchard. Micky waited at table with his hat on, and then disappeared for awhile. At two o'clock he rose again above the horizon, and said that the electric car was at the door. Richard and Teresa set off to meet the two-thirty train at Leighton Buzzard. By this time they had certainly become rather intimate, according to the way of young persons thrown together—by no matter what chance—in the month of June—or any other month. It was not, perhaps, unnatural that Raphael Craig, when he emerged from the railway station and found the two laughing and chatting side by side in the motor-car, should have cast at them a sidelong glance, in which were mingled amusement, alarm, and warning.

Mr. Raphael carried the large brown portmanteau, which was now—as Richard discovered by handling it—quite empty. On the journey home Teresa drove the car, and her father sat by her

side. Richard occupied the rear of the car, giving
a hint occasionally as to the management of the
machine.

'I think I have nothing further to do here,'
he said, when the party had arrived safely at
Queen's Farm. 'Both the other cars are in order.
I will therefore bid you good-day. Should anything
go wrong with this car, you will doubtless let us
know.'

He spoke in his most commercial manner, though
his feelings were far from commercial. Raphael
Craig bent those dark, deep eyes of his upon the
youth.

'I have been telephoning to your firm this morning,' said Craig, 'and have arranged with them
that you shall take the Panhard back to town.
They are going to take it off my hands—at a
price.'

'With pleasure,' said Richard.

'But,' Mr. Craig continued, 'I wish to use the
Panhard this week-end. Therefore you cannot
remove it till Monday.'

'Very good,' said Richard, 'I will present myself
on Monday morning.'

'And in the meantime?'

'In the meantime I have other business for my
firm in the neighbourhood.'

Teresa's glance intercepted her father's, and
these two exchanged a look. The old man frowned
at his daughter.

'Good-day,' said Richard.

Raphael and Teresa shook hands with him. Was he a conceited ass, or did Teresa really seem aggrieved?

'Till Monday,' said Teresa.

Richard walked down to the village, engaged Miss Puddephatt's room, and dined at the White Horse Hotel. He had not yet definitely decided what course of conduct to follow. He was inclined to do nothing further in the affair, and to tell Simon Lock on Monday that, so far as he could discover, Simon Lock's suspicions about Raphael Craig were groundless. He had taken no money from Simon Lock, and he would take none. Yet why should he pause now? Why should he not, for his own private satisfaction, probe the mystery to the bottom? Afterwards—when the strange secret stood revealed to him—there would be plenty of time then to decide whether or not to deliver up Richard Craig into the hands of Simon Lock. Yes, on consideration he would, for his own pleasure, find out whatever was to be found out.

That evening, an hour after sunset, he lay hidden behind a hedge on the west side of Watling Street, exactly opposite the boreen leading to the Queen's Farm.

Richard slept. He was decidedly short of sleep, and sleep overtook him unawares. Suddenly from the end of the boreen came the faint spit, spit of a motor-car, growing louder as it approached the main road. Would it awake Richard? No, he slept stolidly on. The motor-car, bearing an old

man and a young girl, slid down into the valley
towards Dunstable, and so out of hearing. An
hour passed. The church clock at Houghton
Regis, two miles off to the east, struck midnight.
Then the car might have been heard returning.
It laboured heavily up the hill, and grunted as
though complaining of its burden as it curved
round into the boreen towards Queen's Farm.

Richard awoke. In a fraction of a second he
was wide awake, alert, eager, excited. He saw
the car vanishing towards the outbuildings of
Queen's Farm. Springing out of the hedge, he
clambered over the opposite hedge into Craig's
orchard, crossed it, passed the house by its north
side, and so came to the quadrangle of outbuildings.
By keeping on the exterior of this quadrangle he
arrived at last, skirting the walls, at the blind end
of the boreen. He peeped cautiously round the
angle of the wall, scarcely allowing even the tip
of his nose to protrude, and discerned the empty
motor-car. He ventured forward into the boreen.
It was at this corner of the quadrangle that the
locked shed was situated. Rather high up in the
wall a light disclosed the presence of a small window.
The faintness of the light proved that the window
must be extremely dirty. But even if it had been
clean he could not have utilised it, for it was seven
feet from the earth. He put his hand on the wall
and touched a spout. The spout felt rickety, but
he climbed up it, and, clinging partly to the spout
and partly to the frame of the window, he looked

into the locked shed. It had once, he perceived,
been used as a stable, but it was being put to other
purposes now. The manger was heaped up with
bright silver coins. In the middle of the floor stood
a large iron receptacle of peculiar shape. He
guessed that it had been constructed to fit into
the well of the Panhard motor-car. By means of
two small buckets Teresa and her father were trans-
ferring the contents of this receptacle, which was
still half full of silver, into the manger.

The shed was lighted by a single candle stuck
insecurely on what had once been a partition between two stalls. The candle flickered and cast
strange shadows. The upper part of the chamber
was in darkness. Looking straight across it,
Richard saw another little window exactly opposite his own; and through this window he discerned
another watching face.

'Micky!' he exclaimed softly to himself.

Raphael and Teresa were, then, doubly spied
upon. But who was Micky?

Richard's attention was diverted from this interesting inquiry by the gradual growth of a light
near the door, of which, being parallel with his
window, he had no view. Then a long, licking
flame appeared. He could see it creeping across
the floor, nearer and nearer to the unconscious
heavers of silver. Raphael had turned on the
waste tap of the exhaust petrol under the motor-
car. The highly combustible liquid had run beneath
the door of the shed and had there come in contact

with the wax match used by Raphael to light the candle and then thrown down. Richard saw next that the door of the shed was on fire; at the same moment, unable any longer to keep his grip on the spout and the window-frame, he fell unexpectedly to the ground.

CHAPTER VI

THE DESIRE FOR SILVER

THE blazing door was locked. Richard called, shouted, shouted again. There was no answer, but in the extraordinary outer silence he could still hear the industrious shovelling of silver.

'Well,' he said to himself, 'they're bound to find out pretty soon that the show's on fire.'

He threw himself against the door angrily, and, to his surprise, it yielded, and he fell over the river of flame into the interior of the shed. The noise at last startled Raphael and Teresa out of the preoccupation of their task.

'Haven't you perceived that the place is being burned down?' he exclaimed dryly.

At the same instant he sprang towards Teresa. The stream of burning petrol had found its way into the central runnel of the stone floor, and so had suddenly reached the hem of Teresa's dress, which already showed a small blaze. Fortunately, it was a serge travelling frock; had it been of light summer material, Teresa would probably have been burned to death. Richard dragged her fiercely from the region of the runnel, and extinguished the smouldering serge between his hands, which showed the scars of that timely action for a fortnight afterwards. He glanced round quickly, saw a pile of empty sacks in a corner—had they been used as money-bags? he wondered—and, seizing several of them, laid them flat on the burning petrol and against the door. His unhesitating celerity no doubt prevented a magnificent conflagration. The petrol, it is true, had nearly burnt itself out, but the woodwork of the door was, in fireman's phrase, 'well alight,' and, being aged and rotten, it formed a quick fuel.

When the flames had been conquered, the three occupants of the shed looked at each other without a word. Strange to say, under the steady gaze of Raphael Craig, Richard's eyes blinked, and he glanced in another direction—up at the little window in the opposite wall where he had seen the face of Micky, but where the face of Micky was no longer on view. Then he looked again at Raphael Craig, whose dark orbs seemed to ask accusingly: 'What are you doing here?' And, despite the fact that he had in all probability been the means of saving Teresa's life, he could not avoid the absurd sensation of having been caught in a misdeed. He felt as if he must explain his presence to Raphael Craig. At that juncture, we are obliged to confess, his imperturbability deserted him for a space.

'I—I happened to be passing the end of the road,' he said lamely, 'and I saw what I took to be a flame, so I ran along—and found—this. I'm glad it's no worse.'

'So am I,' said Raphael Craig, with cold gravity. Teresa was silent.

"I'm glad I was in time,' said Richard, as awkwardly as a boy.

'I'm glad you were,' Mr. Craig agreed. 'It is possible that my daughter owes her life to you. I cannot imagine how I could have been so careless with that petrol. It was inexcusable. We thank you, Mr. Redgrave, for your services so admirably rendered.'

'Don't mention it,' said Richard; 'that's nothing at all.'

The whole interview was becoming too utterly ridiculous. But what could be said or done? It was the heaps of silver coins lying about that rendered the situation so extremely difficult. Useless for Raphael Craig to pretend that he and Teresa had been engaged in some perfectly usual and common-place task. Useless for Richard, notwithstanding his lame explanation, to pretend that he had not been spying. The heaps of silver made all parties excessively · self-conscious, and when you are self-conscious you can never say the right thing in the right manner.

It was Raphael Craig who first, so to speak, came to himself.

'As you are here, Mr. Redgrave,' he said, 'as you have already laid us under one obligation, perhaps you will consent to lay us under another.

Perhaps you will help us to finish off these few coins. Afterwards I will beg the honour of a few words with you in private.'

It was magnificent, thought Richard, this audacious manœuvre of the old man's. It took the bull by the horns in a very determined fashion. It disarmed Richard instantly. What course, save that of complying with so calm and courteous a request, could he pursue? He divined that Raphael Craig was not a man moulded to the ordinary pattern of bank managers.

'With pleasure,' he replied, and thereupon the heaps of silver seemed less bizarre, less confusing, less productive of a general awkwardness. By a fiction unanimously agreed to, all three began to behave as if shovelling thousands of new silver coins at dead of night in a disused stable was a daily affair with them.

Still without uttering a word, Teresa handed her galvanised iron bucket to Richard. He noticed a little uncertainty in the motion of her hand as she did so. The next moment there was a thud on the floor of the stable. Teresa had fainted. She lay extended on the stone floor. Richard ran to pick up that fair frame. He had lifted the girl's head when the old man interposed.

'Never raise the head of a person who has lost consciousness,' he said coldly; 'it is dangerous. Teresa will recover in a few minutes. This swoon is due only to the shock and strain of the last few minutes. In the meantime, will you open the door?'

Richard, having complied, stood inactive, anxious to do something, yet finding nothing to do.

'Shall I fetch some water from the house?' he asked. 'Swoons are sometimes very serious if they last too long.'

'Are they, my friend?' said Raphael, with the trace of a smile. 'This one is already over—see?'

Teresa opened her eyes.

'What are you two staring at?' she inquired curiously, and then sighed as one fatigued.

Her father raised her head in his arm and held it so for a few moments.

'Now, my chuck,' he said, 'try if you can stand. Mr. Redgrave, will you assist me?'

Mr. Redgrave assisted with joy. The girl at length stood up, supported on one side by Raphael Craig and on the other by the emissary of Simon Lock. With a glance at Richard, she said she could walk. Outside stood the motor-car.

'Shall we take her round to the front-door on this?' Richard suggested.

'Are you mad?' exclaimed Raphael Craig, with sudden disapproval. 'Teresa will walk.'

He locked the charred door of the stable with a padlock which he took from his pocket, and they proceeded to the house.

Bridget stood at the front-door, seeming to expect them.

'You're not well, mavourneen,' she said, glancing at Teresa's face, and led the girl away. During the whole of the time spent by him at Queen's

Farm nothing impressed Richard more than the impassive yet affectionate demeanour of Mrs. Bridget, that mysterious old servant, on this occasion.

The two men were left together in the hall. Mrs. Bridget and Teresa had gone upstairs.

'Mike!' Raphael Craig called.

'Yes, sorr,' answered Mike, appearing from a small butler's pantry under the staircase.

'Bring whisky into the drawing-room.'

'That I will, sorr.'

Richard admired Micky's sangfroid, which was certainly tremendous, and he determined to have an interview with the man before many hours were past, in order to see whether he could not break that sangfroid down.

'Come into the drawing-room, will you?' said Raphael Craig.

'Thanks,' said Richard.

The drawing-room proved to be the room into which Mr. Craig had vanished on the previous night. It presented, to his surprise, no unusual feature whatever. It had the customary quantities of chairs, occasional tables, photographs, knick-knacks, and cosy corners. It was lighted by a single lamp suspended from the middle of the ceiling. The only article of furniture that by any stretch of fancy could be termed extraordinary in a drawing-room was a rather slim grandfather's clock in an inlaid case of the Sheraton period. This clock struck one as they went into the room.

Micky arrived with the whisky.

'You will join me?' asked Raphael, lifting the decanter.

'Thanks,' said Richard.

'That will do, Mike.'

Mike departed. The two men ignited cigars and drank. Each was seated in a large easy-chair.

'Now for it,' said Richard to himself.

Mr. Raphael Craig coughed.

'I dare say, Mr. Redgrave,' the bank manager began, 'that certain things which you have seen this evening will have struck you as being some-what strange.'

'I am happy to have been of any help,' said Richard.

Raphael bowed.

'I will not disguise from you,' he continued, 'that when you arrived here in such a peculiar manner last night I had my suspicions of your good faith. I even thought for a moment—it was very foolish of me—that you were from Scotland Yard. I don't know why I should have thought that, but I did think it.'

'Really,' said Richard, 'I have not the least connection with Scotland Yard. I told you my business.'

'I believe you,' said Raphael. 'I merely mention the course of my thoughts concerning you. I am fully convinced now that, despite certain unusual items connected with your visit, you are exactly what you said you were, and for my doubts I now offer apology. To tell you the truth, I inquired from the Williamson Company this morning as to you, and was quite reassured by what they said. But,' Mr. Craig went on, with a very pronounced 'but,' interrupting Richard, who had embarked on some protest—'but I have at the same time been forced to the conclusion, Mr. Redgrave, that my household, such as it is, and my ways, such as they are, have roused in you a curiosity which is scarcely worthy of yourself. I am a fairly good judge of character, and I know by infallible signs that you have a nature far above idle curiosity.'

'Thanks for your good opinion,' said Richard; 'but, to deal with your suspicions in their order, may I ask why you thought at first that I was an agent of Scotland Yard? Were you expecting Scotland Yard at Queen's Farm?'

He could not avoid a faint ironic smile.

Mr. Craig threw his cigar into the fireplace.

'I was,' said Raphael briefly, 'and I will tell you why. Some time ago an uncle of mine died, at a great age, and left me a huge fortune. My uncle, Mr. Redgrave, was mad. For fifty years he had put all his savings into silver coins. He had once been in a Mexican silver-mine, and the experience in some mysterious way had affected his brain. Perhaps his brain was already affected. He lived for silver, and in half a century he collected more than half a million separate silver coins— all English, all current, all unused. This fortune he bequeathed to me. I was, in fact, his sole relative.'

'A strange old fellow he must have been,' Richard remarked.

'Yes,' said Raphael. 'But I am equally strange. I have said that my uncle had a mania. I, too, have that mania, for I tell you, Mr. Redgrave, that I cannot bring myself to part with those coins. I have the same madness for silver that my uncle had. Away from the silver, I can see myself steadily, can admit frankly to myself that on that one point my brain is, if you like the term, "touched." In the presence of the silver I exist solely for it, and can think of nothing else.'

'Nevertheless,' said Richard dispassionately, 'I was told in the village to-day that you paid for everything in silver. If you are so attached to silver, how can you bring yourself to part with it? Why not pay in gold?'

'Because,' Raphael replied, 'I never handle gold save in my professional capacity as bank manager. I take my salary in silver. I cannot help it. The weight frequently proves a difficulty, but I cannot help it. Silver I must have. It is in my blood, the desire for silver. True, I pay away silver—simply because I have no other coins available.'

'I see,' said Richard.

He scarcely knew what to think of his strange companion. The man seemed absolutely sane, absolutely in possession of every sense and faculty, yet, behold him accusing himself of madness!

'Let me finish,' said Raphael Craig. 'When
I came into my uncle's fortune I was at a loss
what to do with it. The small house which I
then had over at Sewell, near Chalk Hill, had no
accommodation for such a valuable and ponderous
collection. I made a confidante of my daughter.
She sympathised with me, and suggested that,
at any rate for a time, I should conceal the hoard
in a disused chalk-pit which lay a few hundred
yards from our house. The idea, at first sight
rather wild, grew upon me. I adopted it. Then
I took this house, and gradually I have removed
my silver from the chalk-pit to Queen's Farm. It
is hidden in various quarters of the place. We
brought the last load to-night.'

'This is very interesting,' said Richard, who had
nothing else to say.

'I have told you this,' the old man concluded,
'in order to account to you for what you saw to-
night in that stable. It is but just that you should
know. I thank you again for your prompt services
in the matter of the fire, and I ask you, Mr. Redgrave, to pity the infirmity—the harmless infirmity
—of an old man.'

Raphael Craig stood up and gazed at Richard
with his deep-set melancholy eyes.

'It is an infirmity which draws suspicion upon
this house as a magnet draws iron. Once already
I have had the local police up here making stupid
inquiries. I put them off as well as I could. Daily
I am expecting that the directors of the bank will

call me up to explain my conduct. Yet I cannot do otherwise.'

'Why,' said Richard, 'if you are rich, do you still care to serve the bank? Pardon my impertinence, but, surely, if you left the bank one source of your apprehensions would be stopped?'

'I cannot leave the bank,' said Raphael Craig, with solemn pathos; 'it would break my heart.'

With these words he sank back into a chair, and appeared to be lost in thought. So the two sat for some time. Then Richard rose and went quietly towards the door.

'You are the only person, save Teresa, who knows my secret. Remember that, Mr Redgrave.'

The manager's voice sounded weak and distant. Richard bowed and stole from the room. He sucked at his cigar, but it had gone out.

CHAPTER VII

NOLAN

VERY quietly he sauntered to the front-door, which was ajar, and into the portico. He stood there meditating. In front he could vaguely discern the forms of the trees in the orchard, but beyond these nothing. The night was as dark as a wolf's mouth. Then the sound of a horse's rapid hoof caught his ear. The wind had fallen, and everything was still. Looking down the hill, he could see the light of a vehicle ascending the slope of Watling Street. The sound of the horse's trot came nearer and nearer, passed the end of the boreen, and so continued up the hill, getting fainter now, till it died entirely away as the vehicle dipped down the gradient into Hockliffe. The vehicle was one of her late Majesty's mails, which took that route at that hour on Saturday nights only. It constituted a perfectly simple weekly phenomenon, yet somehow the birth, growth, fading, and death of the sound of the horse's trot on the great road affected Richard's imagination to a singular degree.

'What is my position up here now?' he asked himself. 'Am I to depart an unconfessed spy, without another word to Raphael Craig or Teresa, or—what?'

The old man's recital had touched him, and Teresa's swoon had decidedly touched him more.

He strolled very leisurely down the drive, staring about him. Then, with senses suddenly alert, he whispered:

'Come out, there. I see you quite well.'

Micky was hiding in the bushes under the drawing-room window. The little man obeyed complacently enough.

'Come out into the road with me, Mike; I want to have a chat with you.'

Richard had sufficient tact not to put any sign of reproof or anger into his tone. He accepted Micky's spying as a thing of course. They walked along the boreen together and up the high-road towards Hockliffe.

'Now,' said Richard, 'we can talk at our ease here; we shan't be overheard.'

'What does your honour want to talk about?' asked Micky, with a great air of inno-cence.

'You can drop the "your honour," and all that rigmarole, my friend, and tell me who you really are. To prevent any unnecessary untruths, I may as well tell you at the start that I found Goron's Memoirs in the pocket of your coat in the harness-room yesterday morning. From that moment I knew you were playing a part here.'

'Like you,' said Micky quickly.

'Yes—if it pleases you—like me. What I want to know is, are you a detective?'

'And what I want to know is,' said Micky, who had abandoned most of his Irish accent, 'what are you?'

'Let us not beat about the bush,' said Richard impatiently. 'You're a decent chap, so am I. I will begin by confessing that I am a private inquiry agent employed by the British and Scottish Bank.'

'Oh,' said Micky, 'I knew it was something of that sort. Have you ever heard of a detective named Nolan?'

'What! *the* Nolan?' asked Richard.

'The same,' said Micky.

'You are Nolan?'

'I have the honour—or the dishonour.'

'I am glad to meet you' said Richard. 'Of course, I know you well by reputation. How thoroughly you go into an affair! Fancy you acting as odd man here for weeks! I tell you you have completely imposed on them.'

'Have I?' exclaimed Micky—or Nolan, as he must now be called. 'I should be glad to be assured of that. Twice to-day I have feared that Raphael Craig had his doubts of me.'

'I don't think so for a moment,' said Richard

positively. 'But what is your object—what is Scotland Yard after? Personally, I came here without any theories, on the chance of something turning up.'

'Scotland Yard is merely curious about the suicide—if it was a suicide—of a man named Featherstone, and about the plague of silver which has visited this district during the last year or two.'

'You say "if it was a suicide." Do you suspect that Featherstone's death was due to anything else?'

'I never suspect until I know, Mr. Redgrave. I am here with an open mind.'

'And what have you discovered so far?' asked Richard.

'My very dear sir,' Nolan expostulated, 'what do you take me for? I am sure that you are a man of unimpeachable honour—all private agents are—but, nevertheless, I cannot proclaim my discoveries to a stranger. It would be a breach of etiquette to do so, even if such a course were not indiscreet.'

'I give you my word, Mr. Nolan, that my activity in this case is now entirely at an end. I have found out this evening all that I wished to know, and perhaps more than I wished to know. I shall return to town on Monday morning, and Bedfordshire will know me no more.' He paused, and added: 'At least, it will know me no more as a private inquiry agent.'

'Or a motor-car expert,' said Nolan.

Richard laughed.

'I was merely asking you,' Richard resumed, 'how far you had got, in the hope that possibly I might be able to simplify matters for you.'

'You are very good,' said Nolan, with an indescribable accent of irony—a bantering tone which, however, was so good-humoured that Richard could not take exception to it—'you are very good.'

'You have found out, I presume, something concerning the chalk-pit?'

'Oh yes,' said Nolan, 'I have found out something concerning the chalk-pit.'

'And you know what the crash was early this morning?'

'I have a notion,' said Nolan.

'And, since I saw your inquisitive face at the window of that stable to-night, you know what that stable contains?'

'Not quite to half-a-crown,' said Nolan, 'but approximately.'

'By the way,' Richard asked, 'why on earth didn't you come and assist in putting out the fire?'

'What! And give myself away?'

'It might have been a matter of life and death.'

'Yes, it might have been. Had it got so far, I dare say I should have sacrificed my standing

here, my reputation with these people as a simple
Irishman, in order to save them. But I knew that
you were there, and that you would do all that
was necessary.'

'I only just got into the place in time,' said
Richard sharply.

'Yes. It is a pity that you burned your
hands.'

'How do you know that I burnt my hands?'
Richard asked.

'I can tell by the way you hold them,' said
Nolan.

'It was worth it,' said Richard.

'Was it?' observed Nolan quietly. 'I am
glad. Of course, now that you have found
out everything——'

He drew up standing in the road. His voice
showed that Richard had made some little
impression on that great man from Scotland
Yard.

'Admit first,' said Richard, his eyes twinkling
through the gold-rimmed spectacles, 'that you
were guilty of the grossest indiscretion—not to say
stupidity—in leaving Goron's Memoirs, a yellow-
covered French book, lying about the harness-room
—you, an Irish labourer.'

'I admit that in that matter I was an inconceivable ass,' said Nolan cheerfully.

'Good!' said Richard; 'you shall have your
reward.'

Then Richard told him all that he had learnt

from the lips of Raphael Craig. There was a silence when he had finished.

'Yes,' said Nolan, 'it's rather an impressive story; it impresses even me. But do you believe it?'

'I believe what Craig told me. If he lied, he is the finest actor I ever saw.'

'Listen,' said Nolan. 'Does this tale of Craig's explain his daughter's visit to Bosco's circus and her chat with Juana, and her unblushing fibs to you afterwards?'

'How did you hear about that?' questioned Richard savagely.

He scarcely liked Nolan's curt language in regard to Teresa.

'I did hear about it,' said Nolan; 'let that suffice. And listen further. I will make you a present of a fact—an absolutely indisputable fact —which I have discovered: Raphael Craig never had an uncle. His father was an only son. Moreover, no person has died within the last few years who could by any means be related to Craig. The records at Somerset House have been thoroughly searched.'

'No uncle!' was all Richard, the nonplussed, could murmur.

'And,' Nolan continued, 'while I am about it, I will make you a present of another little fact. You say that Craig told you that he had brought all his silver here, the last load having arrived to-night. On the contrary, he has gradually been taking silver away from here. I admit that he has brought some, but he has carted far more away. For what else should he need all this generous supply of motor-cars?'

Richard began to suspect that he had mistaken his vocation.

CHAPTER VIII

THE PEER'S ADVICE

ON the Monday morning Richard presented himself at Queen's Farm. The day was jocund, the landscape smiled; in the forty-acre field below the house a steam-plough, actuated by two enormous engines and a steel hawser, was working at the bidding of a farmer who farmed on principles of his own, and liked to do his ploughing at mid-summer. The steam-plough rattled and jarred and jolted like a humorous and high-spirited leviathan; the birds sang merrily above it; the Chiltern Hills stretched away in the far distance, bathed in limitless glad sunshine; and Watling Street ran white, dazzling, and serene, down the near slope and up the hill towards Dunstable, curtained in the dust of rural traffic.

In the midst of all these things joyous and content, behold Richard, melancholy and full of discontent, ringing at the front-door bell of Queen's Farm. He rang and rang again, but there was no answer. It was after eight o'clock, yet not a blind had been drawn up; and the people of the

house had told him that they took breakfast at
seven o'clock! Richard had passed a wretched
week-end in the village of Hockliffe, his one solace
having been another chat with Mr. Puddephatt,
wine-merchant and horse-dealer to the nobility
and gentry of the neighbourhood. He was at a
loss what to do. What, indeed, could he do? The
last words of Nolan, the detective, had given him
pause, hinting, as they did, at strange mysteries
still unsolved. Supposing that he, Richard, continued his investigations and discovered some
sinister secret—some crime? The point was that
Teresa was almost certainly involved in her father's
schemes. Here was the difficulty which troubled
him. His fancy pictured a court of justice, and
Raphael Craig and Teresa in the dock, and Richard
Redgrave giving evidence against them, explaining
how he had spied upon them, dogged their footsteps, and ultimately arrived at the heart of the
mystery. Could he do that? Could he look Teresa
in the face? And yet, what, after all, was Teresa
to him—Teresa, whom he had known only three
days?

That was the question—what was Teresa to
him?

He rang again, and the jangle of the bell rever-
berated as though through a deserted dwelling.
Then he walked round the house by the garden,
in the hope of encountering Micky, otherwise Mr.
Nolan of Scotland Yard. But not a sign of Mr.
Nolan could he see anywhere. The stable-door

was unlocked; the mares were contentedly at work on a morning repast of crushed oats, followed by clover-hay, but there was no Micky. He began to think that perhaps Nolan knew a great deal more than he had chosen to tell during that night walk along Watling Street. Perhaps Nolan had returned to Scotland Yard armed with all the evidence necessary to conduct a magnificent *cause célèbre* to a successful conclusion. He could see the posters of the evening papers: 'Extraordinary Affair in Bedfordshire: A Bank Manager and his Daughter charged with——' Charged with what?

Pooh! When he recalled the dignified and absolutely sincere air of Raphael Craig at their interview in the drawing-room in the early hours of Sunday morning, when he recalled the words of the white-haired man, uttered with an appealing glance from under those massive brows: 'I ask you, Mr. Redgrave, to pity the infirmity, the harmless infirmity, of an old man'—when he recalled these words, and the manner of the speaker, he could not but think that Nolan must be on an absolutely false scent; he could not but believe that the Craigs were honest and innocent.

He at last got round to the kitchen-door of the house and knocked. The door was immediately opened—or, rather, half opened—by Mrs. Bridget, who put her head in the small aperture thus made after the manner of certain women. She merely looked at him severely, without uttering a word.

'I wish to see Mr. Craig,' he said calmly.

'I was to tell ye the motor-car is in the shed, and ye are kindly to deliver it at Williamson's.'

This was her reply.

'Mr. Craig is not up then? Miss Craig——'

'I was to tell ye the motor-car is in the shed, and ye are kindly to deliver it at Williamson's.'

'Thank you. I perfectly understand,' said Richard. 'Miss Craig, I hope, is fully recovered?'

'I was to tell ye the motor-car——'

Thinking that this extraordinary Irishwoman was scarcely in full possession of her wits that morning, Richard turned away, and proceeded to the shed where the motor-cars were kept. The Panhard, he found, was ready for action, its petrol-tank duly filled, its bearings oiled, its brasswork polished. He sprang aboard and set off down the boreen. As he passed the house, gazing at it, one of the drawn blinds on the first-floor seemed to twitch aside and then fall straight again. Or was it his imagination?

He turned into Watling Street, and then, on the slope, set the car to its best pace. He reached the valley in a whirl of dust at a speed of forty miles an hour. The great road stretched invitingly ahead. His spirits rose. He seemed to recover somewhat from the influence of the mysteries of Queen's Farm.

'I'll chuck it,' he shouted to himself above the
noise of the flying car—'that's what I'll do. I'll
go and tell Lord Dolmer this very morning that
I can't do anything, and prefer to waste no more
time on the affair.'

After that he laughed, also to himself, and
swerved the car neatly to avoid half a brick which
lay in the middle of the road. It was at that moment
that he perceived, some distance in front, his friend
Mr. Puddephatt. Mr. Puddephatt was apparently
walking to Dunstable. Richard overtook him and
drew up.

'Let me give you a lift,' said Richard.

Mr. Puddephatt surveyed the Panhard askance.

'Let me give you a lift?' Mr. Puddephatt repeated. It was his habit to repeat the exact words
of an interlocutor before giving a reply. 'No,
thanks,' said he. 'I'm walking to Dunstable Station
for exercise.'

'What are you going to Dunstable Station for?'
asked Richard.

'I'm for Lunnon—horse sale at the Elephant
and Castle. Perhaps you know the Elephant and
Castle, sir?'

'I'll give you a lift to London, if you like,' said
Richard, seizing the chance of companionship, of
which he was badly in need. 'We shall get there
quite as soon as your train.'

Mr. Puddephatt eyed the car suspiciously. He
had no sympathy with motor-cars.

'Are you afraid?' asked Richard.

'Am I afraid?' he repeated. 'No,' he said, 'I ain't afraid. But I'd sooner be behind a three-year-old than behind one of them things. But I'll try it and see how I like it. And thank ye, sir.'

So Mr. Puddephatt journeyed with Richard to London.

Perhaps it was fate that induced Mr. Puddephatt, when they had discussed the weather, horses, motor-cars, steam-ploughs, wine, parish councils, London, and daily papers, to turn the conversation on to the subject of the Craigs. Mr. Puddephatt had had many and various dealings with the Craigs, and he recounted to Richard the whole of them, one after another, in detail. It seemed, from his narrative, that he had again and again, from sheer good-nature, saved the Craigs from the rapacity and unscrupulousness of the village community.

'Nice young lady, that Miss Teresa,' observed Mr. Puddephatt.

'Yes,' said Richard.

By this time they had passed through St. Albans and were well on the way to Edgware.

'They do say,' said Mr. Puddephatt, leaning back luxuriously against the cushions—'they do say as she isn't his daughter—not rightly.'

'They sat what?' asked Richard quietly, all alert, but not choosing to seem so.

Mr. Puddephatt reaffirmed his statement.

'Who says that?' asked Richard.

'Oh!' said Mr. Puddephatt, 'I dare say it isn't true. But it's gotten about the village. Ye never know how them tales begin. I dare say it isn't true. Bless ye, there's lots o' tales.'

'Oh, indeed!' Richard remarked sagaciously.

'Ay!' said Mr. Puddephatt, filling his pipe, 'lots o' tales. That night as she ran away from the farm, and Mrs. Bridget had to fetch her back from the White Horse—— Everybody said as how the old man ill-treated her, daughter or no daughter.'

'When was that?'

'A few weeks back,' said Mr. Puddephatt laconically.

This was all he would say.

'It's a queer world, Mr. Puddephatt,' said Richard aloud. To himself he said: 'Then perhaps she isn't involved with her father—if he is her father.'

At length they reached the suburbs of London and had to moderate their speed. As they wound in and out through the traffic of Kilburn, Richard's eye chanced to catch the sign of the British and Scottish Bank. He drew up opposite the mahogany doors of the bank and, leaving Mr. Puddephatt in charge of the car, entered. It was turned ten o'clock. He felt fairly certain that Raphael Craig had not left Queen's Farm, but he wanted to convince himself that the bank manager was not always so impeccably prompt at business as some people said.

'I wish to see Mr. Craig,' he said, just as he had said two hours before to Mrs. Bridget.

'Mr. Craig,' said the clerk, 'is at present taking his annual holiday. He will return to business in a fortnight's time.'

Richard returned to the car curiously annoyed, with a sense of being baffled. His thoughts ran back to Teresa. Thirty miles of Watling Street now separated them, yet her image was more strenuously before him than it had been at any time since she fainted in the silver-heaped stable on Saturday night.

'Yes,' he said to himself positively, 'I'll call on Lord Dolmer at once, and tell him I won't have anything further to do with the affair.'

He dropped Mr. Puddephatt, whose society, he felt, was perhaps growing rather tedious to him, at Oxford Circus, and directed him to an omnibus for the Elephant and Castle.

'My address is 4, Adelphi Terrace, in case you need a friend in London at any time,' said Richard.

'Good-day to ye, sir,' said Mr. Puddephatt, 'and thank ye kindly. Shall we be seeing you again at Hockliffe soon?'

'No,' said Richard shortly. 'I am not likely ever to come to Hockliffe. My business there is absolutely concluded.'

They shook hands, full of goodwill. As Mr. Puddephatt's burly and rustic form faded away into the crowd Richard watched it, and thought

how strange, and, indeed, pathetic, it was that
two human beings should casually meet, become
in a measure intimate, and then part for evermore,
lost to each other in the mazy wilderness of an
immense civilisation.

He drove the car to Holborn Viaduct, deposited
it on the Williamson Company's premises, and
then took a bus for Piccadilly. As he did so it
began to rain, at first gently, then with a more
determined steadiness: a spell of fine weather
which had lasted for several weeks was at last
broken.

In less than half an hour he was at Lord Dolmer's
door in Half Moon Street.

This nobleman, as has been stated, was comparatively a poor man. Emphasis must now be
laid on that word 'comparatively.' The baron
had a thousand a year of his own in stocks, and a
small property in Yorkshire which brought in a
trifle less than nothing a year, after all the out-
goings were paid. His appointments in the City
yielded him fifteen hundred a year. So that his
net income was a trifle less than two thousand five
hundred pounds per annum. He was thus removed from the fear of absolute starvation. The
peerage was not an ancient one—Lord Dolmer
was only the second baron—but the blood was
aristocratic; it had run in the veins of generations
of men who knew how to live and how to enjoy
themselves. Lord Dolmer had discreetly remained
a bachelor, and, in the common phrase, 'he did

D

himself uncommonly well.' He had a suite of
finely-furnished rooms in Half Moon Street, and
his domestic staff there consisted of a valet, who
was also butler and confidential factotum; a boy,
who fulfilled the functions of a 'tiger,' and
employed his leisure hours in cleaning knives
and boots; a housekeeper, who wore black silk
and guarded the secret of her age; and two
women servants. It was the valet who answered
to Richard's masterful ring; the valet's name was
Simpkin.

'Lord Dolmer at home?' asked Richard.

'Yes, sir,' said Simpkin amicably; 'his lordship
is at breakfast.'

It was just upon eleven o'clock.

'I'll tell him you're here, sir,' said Simpkin.

In another moment Richard was greeting the
second Baron Dolmer in the drawing-room, a
stylish little apartment trimmed with oak. Lord
Dolmer breakfasted in the Continental fashion,
taking coffee at eight, and déjeuner about eleven.
He had the habit of smoking during a meal, and
the border of his plate, which held the remains of
a kidney, showed a couple of cigarette-ends. He
gave Richard a cigarette from his gold case, and
Simpkin supplemented this hospitality with a glass
of adorable and unique sherry.

'We will deprive ourselves of your presence,
Simpkin,' said Lord Dolmer, who, a very simple
and good-natured man at heart, had nevertheless
these little affectations.

'Certainly, sir,' said the privileged Simpkin, who liked to hear his master use these extraordinary phrases.

'And now, Redgrave, what is it? You pride yourself, I know, on your inscrutable features, but I perceive that there is something up.'

'Well,' said Richard, 'it's about that Craig affair. I thought I'd just call and tell you privately that I can't do anything. I should like, if you and Mr. Lock don't object, to retire from it.'

'Singular!' exclaimed Lord Dolmer mildly—'highly singular! Tell me the details, my friend.'

Richard, rather to his own surprise, began to tell the story, omitting, however, all reference to Micky, the detective.

'And do you believe Mr. Raphael Craig's tale?' asked Lord Dolmer. 'It seems to me scarcely to fit in with some of the facts which you have related.'

Richard took breath.

'No, I don't,' he said plumply.

'And yet you prefer to go no further?'

'And yet I prefer to go no further.'

'And this Teresa, who frequents circuses and chalk-pits, and faints at midnight—what sort of a girl is she?'

'Miss Craig is a very beautiful woman,' said Richard stiffly.

He tried hard to speak in a natural tone of voice, but failed.

'She has bewitched you, Redgrave,' said Lord Dolmer. 'It is a clear case. She has bewitched you. This won't do at all—my unimpressionable Redgrave knocked over by a country girl of nineteen or so!'

He rubbed his hands together, and then lighted another cigarette.

Richard pulled himself together, and replied, smiling:

'Not at all. . . . But really, Lord Dolmer, I want to throw the thing up. So far from Miss Craig having bewitched me, I shall, in all probability, never see her again.'

'I see—a heroic sacrifice! Well, I will tell Mr. Simon Lock . . . what shall I tell him?'

'Tell him I have discovered nothing definite, and own myself beaten as regards finding out the true origin of Raphael Craig's eccentricities. But tell him, also, that I am convinced that Raphael Craig is nothing worse than eccentric.' Richard paused, and repeated: 'Yes, nothing worse than eccentric.'

'No, Redgrave, I won't tell him that you are convinced of that.'

'And why not?'

'Because, forgive me, I am convinced that you are not convinced of it.'

There was an interval of silence, during which two spirals of smoke ascended gracefully to the panelled ceiling of Lord Dolmer's dining-room.

'Perhaps I am not,' Richard answered calmly. 'Tell Simon Lock what you like, then, only make it plain that I retire. I ask no fee, since I have earned none. I wash my hands of the whole business. I am within my rights in so doing.'

'Certainly you are within your rights,' said Lord Dolmer. 'And d'you know, Redgrave, I am rather glad that you are retiring from the case."

'Why?'

'If I tell you my reason you will regard it as strictly confidential?'

Richard assented.

'It is this: Mr. Simon Lock has a mysterious animus against Raphael Craig; what the cause of that animus is neither I nor any of the other directors can guess, but it exists. (Remember, all this is between friends.) It is Mr. Lock who has forced on this secret inquiry. The other directors were against a proceeding which is rather underhand and contrary to the best traditions of the bank. But Mr. Simon Lock had his way.' Here Lord Dolmer lighted another cigarette and resumed. 'I ask you, why should the bank interfere? A bank manager has a perfect right to live where he likes, and, outside office hours, to do what he likes, so long as he obeys the laws of the country and the laws of respectability. Mr. Lock laid stress on the fact that Raphael Craig had been fined for furious motor-car driving. But what of that? It is a misfortune which may overtake the wisest of us. You, my dear Redgrave, well know that even I have several times only narrowly escaped the same ignominious fate. The fact is—and I tell you this candidly—there is something between Mr. Simon Lock and Raphael Craig. When Mr. Lock joined the Board one of his first actions was to suggest that Craig should be asked to resign—why, no one knows. Craig is one of the most able bank managers in London. He would long since have been promoted to a superior post but for Mr. Simon Lock's consistent opposition. For these reasons, as I say, I am glad that you have retired from the case. For anything I know Raphael Craig may be one of the biggest scoundrels at large. I don't care. The point is that he has not been fairly treated by us—that is to say, by Simon Lock. I have the honour to be an Englishman, and fair play is my creed.' His lordship was silent for a space, and then he said, by way of finale, 'Of course, I rely absolutely upon your discretion, Redgrave.'

Richard nodded.

'What you say is very interesting,' he remarked. 'It is conceivable, then, that Mr. Lock, not to be daunted by my defection, may insist on employing another private detective?'

'Quite conceivable,' Lord Dolmer admitted.

'In that case,' Richard began, and then stopped.

'What?' asked Lord Dolmer.

'Oh, nothing!' said Richard.

Lord Dolmer smiled, and, still smiling, said: 'One word of advice, my friend: forget her.'

'Why?' Richard questioned absently, and bit his lip.

'Forget her,' repeated the Baron.

CHAPTER IX

A VISIT

WELL, he determined, with the ferocious reso-
luteness of a dogged soul, to follow Lord
Dolmer's advice. He said to himself that there
ought to be no special difficulty in doing so, since
only three days had passed since he first saw this
creature whom he was enjoined to forget. He
walked slowly along Piccadilly, down Regent
Street, and through Trafalgar Square to his little
office in Adelphi Terrace. Some trifling business
awaited him there, and this occupied him till the
hour of luncheon. He then went out and lunched,
as his custom was, at Gatti's.

Richard's usual mode of life was extremely
simple. His office, a single small room, was on
the third-floor of No. 4, Adelphi Terrace. On
the fourth-floor he had a bedroom, rather larger
than the office, and quite commodious enough for
the uses of a young bachelor who had no fancy
tastes. When occasion needed he used the office
as a sitting-room. All his meals he took out of
doors. His breakfasts, which cost him fourpence,
he consumed at a vegetarian restaurant hard by;
his luncheons and dinners were eaten at Gatti's.

Frequently at the latter establishment he would be content with a dish of macaroni and half a pint of bitter, at an expenditure of eight-pence—a satisfying repast. His total expenses were thus very small, and hence, although his income was irregular and fluctuating, he nevertheless continually saved money. It was seldom that less than one hundred pounds stood between him and the workhouse. In case of necessity he could have lived for a whole year, or even two years, on one hundred pounds. So he was always in an independent position. He could always afford not to bend his knee to any employer or client. He was, in fact, just what he looked, a shrewd and confident man, successful and well dressed, who knew how to take care of himself. He spent more on his wardrobe than on anything else, and this, not because he was a coxcomb, but from purely commercial motives. He accepted the world as he found the world, and he had learnt that clothes counted.

All afternoon he did nothing but idle about in his office, wondering whether by that time Lord Dolmer had told Simon Lock of the barren result of his inquiries, and wondering also what the upshot of their interview would be. At seven he dined at Gatti's. At eight he returned to Adelphi Terrace, and ascended directly to his bedroom. Opening the window wide, he placed an easy-chair in front of it, lighted a pipe, and sat down to perpend upon things in general.

Richard had chosen this bedroom because of its
view. It looked out at an angle on the river
Thames, stateliest and most romantic of busy
streams. It is doubtful if any capital in Europe,
unless it be Buda-Pesth, the twin city on the blue
Danube, can show a scene equal in beauty to the
Thames Embankment and the Thames when the
hues and mysteries of sunset are upon them.
This particular evening was more than commonly
splendid, for after a day of heavy rain the clouds
had retreated, and the sun burst out in richest
radiance. The red jury-sails of the barges as they
floated up-stream with the flowing tide took on the
tints of the ruby. The vast masonry of Waterloo
Bridge and of Somerset House seemed like gigantic
and strange temples uncannily suspended over
the surface of the glooming water. In the west
Westminster Bridge and the Houses of Parliament
stood silhouetted in profound black against the
occidental sky. The sky was like Joseph's coat
there, but in the east it was like a maiden's scarf.

Up from the Embankment rose the hum and
roar and rattle of London's ceaseless traffic. The
hansoms had lighted their starry lamps, and they
flitted below like fireflies in the shadows of a wood.
No stranger could have guessed that they were
mere hackney vehicles plying at the fixed rate of
two miles for one shilling, and sixpence for every
subsequent mile or part of a mile.

'Yes,' Richard mused, 'this is all very well, and
I am enjoying it, and nothing could be very much

better; but the fact remains that I haven't earned a cent this blessed day. The fact also remains that I am a bit of a frost. Further, and thirdly, the fact remains that the present state of affairs must be immediately altered.'

His pipe went out.

'I'll look in at the Empire,' he said.

Now, by what process of reasoning a young man, who, on his own confession, had drawn a blank day could arrive at the conclusion that the proper thing to do was to go to the Empire we cannot explain. But so it was. He looked at his watch. The hour was nine-fifteen. Half an hour yet, for no self-respecting man-about-town ever thinks of entering the Empire before a quarter to ten! At this point Richard probably fell into a doze. At any rtae, a knock on his bedroom-door had to be repeated several times before it attracted his attention.

'What is it?' he answered at length.

'A person to see you, sir,' said a feminine voice, not without asperity.

'A person to see me! Oh! ah! er! . . . Show him into the office. I'll be down directly.'

He descended to the third-floor, and, instead of the Somerset House acquaintance whom he had expected, he found the very last person that by all the laws of chance ought to have been in his office—he found Mrs. Bridget.

Mrs. Bridget turned round and faced him as he went into the little paper-strewn room. She was dressed in black alpaca, with a curiously-shaped flat black bonnet. Her hands, which were decently covered with black gloves, she held folded in front of her.

Richard said nothing at first. He was too astounded, and—shall we say?—pleased. He scented what the reporters call 'further revelations' of an interesting nature.

'Good-avenin',' said Bridget; 'and can ye see a lady privately?'

'Certainly,' said Richard, 'I can see you privately; but,' he added, with a mischievous smile, 'I'm afraid our interview won't amount to much unless you're more communicative than you were this morning.'

'Bless and save ye, sir! 'tis not meself that wants ye—'tis her.'

'Her?'

'The misthress sent me up to find out whisht whether ye could be seen.'

'Miss Craig is outside?'

'The same, sir. Ye'll see her?'

'See her? Naturally I will see her. But—but —how did you discover my address?'

By this time they were hurrying down the multitudinous steps to the ground-floor.

'Sure, we called at the Williamson Company, and they said you'd left and they didn't know your address. And then we came out, and who should we see but Mr. Puddephatt leading a pony. 'Twas the Virgin's own miracle! "Hullo!" he says, lifting his hat. "Puddephatt," says my mistress——'

The recital was never finished, for at that moment they reached the front-door. In the roadway stood the Décauville motor with lights gleaming. By the side of the Décauville stood Teresa Craig enveloped in a gray mackintosh.

Richard's face showed his intense pleasure at the most unlooked-for encounter.

'Miss Craig,' he said eagerly, 'I hope you are in no trouble. Can I be of any assistance?'

She glanced at him coldly, inimically.

'Mr. Redgrave,' she replied with bitterness, and then looked about—the little street was deserted—'I have come to seek an explanation from you. If you are an honourable man you will give it. And I have come, much against my inclination, to ask a favour. Bridget, take care of the motor.'

She swept imperially before him into the portals of the house.

'Mr. Redgrave,' said Teresa, in a tone which clearly indicated that she meant to lead the conversation, 'we have not seen each other since I was so foolish as to faint in the—the shed.'

They sat together in Richard's little office. It was not without difficulty that he had induced her even to sit down. Her demeanour was hostile. Her fine, imperious face had a stormy and implacable look—a look almost resentful, and Richard felt something of a culprit before that gaze. He met her eyes, however, with such bravery as he could muster.

'Not since then,' he assented. 'I trust you are fully recovered, Miss Craig.'

Ignoring the utterance of this polite hope, she resumed :

'I have to thank you for the service you rendered on Saturday night.'

'It was nothing,' he said, in a voice as cold and formal as her own.

'It was everything,' she corrected him gravely. 'I might have lost my life but for you.'

'I am happy to have been of any assistance,' he said. But his thoughts ran : 'She hasn't come to London to tell me this. What the deuce, then, has she come for?'

'Bridget tells me you had an interview with my father that night. May I ask what passed?' Teresa continued.

'You have not seen your father since then?' said Richard.

'I have not.' Her voice seemed momentarily to break.

'Or doubtless he would have told you?'

'Doubtless.'

Richard determined to try a bold stroke.

'I understood from Mr. Craig that he wished our interview to be strictly confidential.'

'What?' she cried. 'From me? From his daughter?'

She stood up, suddenly angry.

'If, indeed, you are his daughter,' said Richard quietly.

Her eyes blazed, and her hands shook; but she collected herself, and smiled bitterly:

'You, then, have heard that silly rumour?'

'By chance I heard it,' he admitted.

'And you believe it?'

'I neither believe it nor disbelieve it. What has it to do with me?'

'Exactly,' she said; 'a very proper question. What has it to do with you? Listen, Mr. Redgrave. I have the most serious reasons for asking you to tell me what passed between yourself and my father on Saturday night.'

A look of feminine appeal passed swiftly across her features. Fleeting as it was, it sufficed to conquer Richard. A minute ago he had meant to dominate her. Now he was dominated.

'I will tell you,' he said simply, and told her—told her everything without any reservation.

'Then my father did not accuse you of being a professional spy?' she demanded when Richard had finished.

'No,' said Richard, somewhat abashed.

'He did not accuse you of having entered our house under entirely false pretences?'

'No,' said Richard, still more abashed.

There was a silence.

'I wonder,' she said calmly, glancing out of the window, 'I wonder why he did not.'

She made the remark as though she were speculating privately upon a curious but not very important point.

'Miss Craig!' he exclaimed, with an air of being affronted.

'I read in a famous book the other day,' she went on, 'these words: "A murderer is less loathsome to us than a spy. The murderer may have acted on a sudden mad impulse; he may be penitent and amend; but a spy is always a spy, night and day, in bed, at table, as he walks abroad; his vileness pervades every moment of his life."'

'Do you mean to insinuate,' said Richard, forced to defend himself, 'that I am a professional spy?'

'I not only mean to insinuate it, I mean to assert it,' she announced loftily, and then continued more quickly: 'Mr. Redgrave, why did you come to spy on us? For two whole days I trusted you, and I liked you. But that night, as soon as I saw you behind me in the shed, the truth burst upon me. It was that, more than anything else, that caused me to faint. Why did you do it, Mr. Redgrave? My father liked you; I—I—I——' She stopped for a moment. 'Surely a man of your talents could have found a profession more honourable than that of a spy?'

She looked at him, less angry than reproachful.

'I am a private detective,' said Richard sullenly, 'not a spy. My business is perfectly respectable.'

'Why trouble to play with words?' she exclaimed impatiently. 'We took you for a gentle-

man. In our simplicity we took you for a
gentleman.'

'Which I trust I am,' said Richard.

'Prove it!' she cried.

'I will prove it in any manner you choose.'

'I accept your promise,' she said. 'I have
travelled up to London to make an appeal to you
to abandon this inquiry which you have undertaken—at whose instance I know not.'

'I cannot abandon it now,' he said mischiev-
ously.

'Why?' she queried.

'Question for question,' he retorted. 'How did
you discover that I was a professional spy, as you
call it?'

'Bah!' she replied. 'Simply by asking. When
I got your address, the rest was easy. So you
decline to be a gentleman in the manner that I
suggest? I might have anticipated as much. I
might have known that I was coming to London
on a fool's errand. And yet something in your
face hinted to me that perhaps after all——'

'Miss Craig,' he said earnestly, 'I cannot abandon the inquiry now, because I have already
abandoned it. I came down to London this
morning with the intention of doing nothing
more in the matter, and by noon to-day I had
informed my clients to that effect.'

'I was not, then, mistaken in you,' she murmured.

To his intense astonishment there was the tremor
of a sob in that proud voice.

'Not entirely mistaken,' he said, with a faint smile.

'What induced you to give up the business of spying upon us?' she asked, looking at him.

'How can I tell?' he answered; 'conscience, perhaps, though a private detective is not supposed to possess such a thing. Perhaps I did it because I reciprocated your sentiments towards me, Miss Craig.'

'My sentiments towards you?'

'Yes,' he said audaciously. 'You said just now that you liked me.'

Instead of taking offence, she positively smiled. She had the courage of a guileless heart.

'And let me tell you, Miss Craig,' he went on, and his earnestness became passionate, 'that I will do anything that lies in my power to serve you. I don't care what it is. I don't care what trouble you are in; count on me.'

'How do you know that I am in trouble?'

'I don't know,' he said; 'I merely feel it. Miss Craig, let me help you.'

'You don't know what you are saying,' she replied evasively.

He jumped up and seized her hand, her small hand, browned by summer sunshine.

'Let me help you,' he repeated.

'If you knew,' she said, hiding her face, 'what trouble I am in!'

He saw that she was crying. She drew away her hand impulsively.

'I will help you!' he exclaimed; 'the spy, the scorned spy, insists on helping you. Now tell me.'

'Let me go,' she said. 'I came to London to entreat your silence and inaction. I set about the affair in a strange and silly way, but it happens that I have succeeded. You have promised to do nothing further. That suffices. Let me go.'

'You shall not go,' he almost shouted; 'I tell you you shall not go until you have confided in me. I owe you some reparation, and I positively insist on giving it.'

She raised her face and gazed at him.

'I am the child of all misfortune,' she said, 'as my country is the most unfortunate of countries. Mr. Redgrave, my father has disappeared.'

'Oh!' he said, as if to say, 'Is that all?'

'And I dare not search for him.'

'They told me at the bank that he had gone on his annual holiday.'

'Then you inquired at the bank?" she asked swiftly.

'It was my last act of spying,' he said. 'Why dare you not search for your father, Miss Craig?'

'Because—because I might find more than I wished to find.'

'You talk in riddles,' he said firmly. 'We can do nothing here; let us go back to Hockliffe. I will accompany you, and on the way you shall answer my questions. I have many to put to you. Leave everything to me; imagine that I am your brother. I have often laughed at the man's phrase to a woman, "I would lay down my life for you," but at this moment I feel what it means. Do not mistake me; do not think I am talking wildly. Perhaps I have a better idea of your trouble than you think. But, in any case, you must trust me as you trusted me when first you saw me. You must rely on me. Come, let us go.'

She rose and moved towards the door.

'Thanks,' she said, nothing more than that—'thanks.'

In one part of his mind Richard wondered at himself, in another he felt curiously and profoundly happy.

CHAPTER X

MONEY-MAKING

THEY passed northwards through the night of London in the Décauville car, Richard and Teresa side by side on the front seats, old Mrs. Bridget in her black alpaca behind, up Regent Street, along Oxford Street, up the interminable Edgware Road, through Kilburn, and so on to Edgware and the open road and country.

'Bridget knows all my secrets, Mr. Redgrave,' said Teresa. 'Moreover, she has no ears unless I wish it.'

'Sure, miss,' said Bridget, 'more gets into my head than goes out. 'Tis for all the world like a Jew's pocket.'

This fragment of conversation was caused by Richard's sudden stoppage in the middle of a remark about Micky, who, Teresa told him, had disappeared concurrently with her father.

'What were you going to say about Micky?' Teresa asked.

'I was going to say,' Richard answered, 'that things are not what they seem.'

'You mean that Micky, too, was a——'

She hesitated.

'Yes, like me, only rather more professional.'

'Bridget told me this morning that she had heard poor father and Micky at high words in the middle of last night. After that she says there was a silence for a long time, and then father called her up and gave her the message for you.'

The sentences were spoken without hesitation, and yet in a strangely unnatural voice.

'You're forgetting one little thing, miss.'

'Hush, Bridget!' Teresa exclaimed.

'If I am to help you I must be in possession of the facts.'

'Tell him, miss; tell the gintleman, do. The gintleman is a gintleman.'

Teresa sat up straight in the speeding car.

'Yes,' she said, 'you must know. There was a revolver-shot. Bridget says she heard the sound of a revolver-shot. Oh, Mr. Redgrave! what does it mean? I dared not tell you of that before. If my father——'

She ceased.

'Micky has left no trace behind?'

'None.'

'Where did the sound of the shot come from?'

'Sure, from the drawing-room, where the master always kept his pistol-thing in the clockcase. Master and the scoundrel Micky were talking in there.'

'Suppose,' suggested Richard, 'that it was Micky who had a revolver.'

'Then he missed his aim,' said Bridget, 'for the master came to me afterwards on the upper landing as sound as a bell.'

'Did he seem agitated?' Richard asked.

'Not he! Why should a gintleman seem agitated because he has shot a scoundrel?'

Bridget appeared to glory in the idea that Raphael Craig might indeed have shot the Scotland Yard detective.

'And since then you have seen nothing of either your father or Micky?'

'Nothing whatever,' said Teresa.

'And you have no notion where they are?'

'None; at least—no—none.'

'I observed this morning,' said Richard quietly, 'that the new electric car was not in the shed.'

'Sure, and the master must have ridden off on it with the corpse——'

'Bridget, silence!' said Teresa imperatively.

Richard had an uncanny vision of Raphael Craig flying from justice on the electric car, with the corpse of a murdered detective hidden somewhere behind. The vision struck him, though, as amusing. He could not believe in the possibility of such a deed on the part of Raphael Craig. Yet he could see that Bridget's doubtless fanciful and highly-coloured report of what had passed in the night had worked on Teresa's brain, already disturbed by sinister events. He could understand now why she had so incontinently flown to London,

in the wild hope of stopping all further inquiries
into her father's proceedings.

The car climbed over the hill on which stands
the town of St. Albans, and then slipped easily
down towards Redbourne and the twelve miles of
lonely and straight Watling Street that separates
St. Albans from Dunstable. On this interminable
and monotonous stretch of road there are only
two villages; mile succeeds mile with a sort of
dogged persistency, and the nocturnal traveller
becomes, as it were, hypnotised by the ribbon-
like highway that stretches eternally in front of
him and behind him. It was fortunate that the
car ran well. Dunstable was reached in forty
minutes after leaving St. Albans, and then as they
passed into the mysterious cutting—resembling a
Welsh mountain pass—to the north of the ancient
borough, the thoughts of all flew forward to the
empty farmhouse which Teresa and her attendant
had left in the morning. As soon as you emerge
from the cutting you can, in daylight, see Queen's
Farm quite plainly on the opposite slope of the
valley, two miles away. But at night, of course,
you can see nothing of the house of Mr. Raphael
Craig unless it is lighted up.

'Sure, the master's returned!' old Mrs. Bridget
exclaimed.

A light faintly twinkled from the direction of
Queen's Farm.

This simple phenomenon produced its effect on
both Teresa and Richard. The old man had come

back, and one mystery, therefore, would at length
be solved—provided that the old man chose to
open his mouth. The idea of thus approaching a
revelation somehow impressed Raphael Craig's
daughter and her companion with a sense of awe,
a sense almost of fear. They were secretly afraid
lest they might encounter something which it
would have been better not to encounter. Each in
fancy pictured Raphael Craig alone in the house
engaged in a strange business. Each silently asked
the question, 'Where is Micky?' and answered it
with a vague and terrible surmise. The feeling that
Raphael Craig was responsible for the disappearance of Micky grew on Richard especially. At first
he had scouted it, but he gradually persuaded
himself that a man like Raphael Craig was capable
of most things, even to disposing of a detective. If
Raphael Craig had indeed any criminal secret to
hide, and he found out that Micky, a Scotland Yard
detective, was prying into the secret, Richard
guessed that the fate of Micky might hazardously
tremble in the balance.

And another aspect of the affair troubled
Richard.

'If your father has returned,' he said to Teresa,
'how shall I explain my presence, or, rather, how
will you explain it? It seems to me that I scarcely
know myself why I am here with you on this car.
I came on the assumption that your father was
gone. His presence would make me a rather unnecessary item, wouldn't it?'

'Who can tell?' Teresa murmured absently; and Richard was rather chagrined at this peculiar reply.

The car was now down in the lowest part of the valley, and the house for the moment out of sight. When, as the car breasted the hill, the summit of the slope reappeared to the view, there was no light in Queen's Farm; the twinkling illumination was extinguished. Only the plain outline of the house stood faintly visible under the waning moon.

'Perhaps father has gone to bed,' said Teresa, with a desperate affectation of lightness. 'I wonder what he would think when he found the house empty.'

Bridget emitted a weird sound which was between a moan and a groan.

'Happen 'twas a fairy light we saw,' she said, the deep instincts of Celtic superstition always rising thus at the slightest invitation.

The car at length turned into the boreen, and so reached the house. The gate was opened, and Richard dexterously twisted the car into the drive. The house—gaunt, bare, sinister—showed no sign whatever of life. The three occupants of the car descended, and stood for a second within the porch.

'The latch-key, Bridget,' said Teresa curtly.

Bridget produced the latch-key, but on putting it into the keyhole Teresa discovered that the door was already unfastened. A push, and it swung backwards, revealing the gloom of the hall.

'Shall I go first?' said Richard.

'If you please,' Teresa replied eagerly, and Richard stepped within. The women followed.

He struck a match, which revealed a low bookcase to the left, and on this a candle. He lighted the candle.

'Stay here,' he said, 'and I will search the house.'

'Sure,' said Bridget, 'we'll stand or fall together. Where you go, me and the misthress go too.'

Richard could not avoid a smile. Together, then, they searched the house from roof to cellar, and found—nothing at all. Apparently not a single thing had been displaced or touched. What could have been the origin of the light which they had seen? Had Mr. Craig returned only to depart again? They stood in the hall asking these questions, which they were unable to answer. Bridget, however, assured that there was nothing of an unusual nature within the house, recovered her wits, and set to work to light lamps in the hall, drawing-room, and kitchen. Richard and Teresa were alone together in the hall. Richard, glancing idly round, stooped down and picked from the floor a gold-handled riding-whip which lay almost under the bookcase. It was a lady's whip.

'A pretty whip,' he remarked. 'Yours, I suppose?'

Teresa went very white.

'It isn't mine,' she said. 'I've never seen it before. I——'

At that very moment there was the sound of hoofs on the gravel of the drive. Richard started for the door, but Teresa clutched him and held him back with an action almost mechanical. Her eyes showed apprehension, mingled with another feeling which Richard almost thought was joy. The hoofs came up the drive and stopped in front of the door, still ajar. The two within the house could just discern the legs of a horse and the skirt of a riding-habit. The rider jumped down, and then cautiously pushed against the door.

'Juana!' cried Teresa, and rushed into the arms of the newcomer.

Richard at once recognised the equestrian of Bosco's circus—tall, dark, Spanish, alluring, mysterious.

The two girls exchanged a passionate kiss, and then stood apart and gazed at each other. Richard discreetly stepped outside and held the horse's bridle. In this animal he recognised the strawberry-roan mare, also of Bosco's circus. In a moment the two girls came out on to the porch.

'Mr. Redgrave,' said Teresa, 'let me introduce you to my sister. She had called here before, and, finding no one, had left. She came back for her whip. Juana, I am in great trouble. Mr. Redgrave has very kindly come to my assistance.'

Richard bowed.

'Come into the drawing-room,' said Teresa. 'You can tie the mare up to this tree, Juana. I expect she won't mind the car.'

When they were all seated in the drawing-room Richard immediately perceived that the two girls meant, at any rate partially, to make a confidant of him. They talked quite openly before him.

'Suppose father should come in?' said the circus-girl.

'You must hide,' said Teresa positively, and, turning to Richard, she went on: 'Mr. Redgrave, my father has not seen my sister for many months, and there are reasons why he should not see her now. You will understand——'

'Perfectly,' assented Richard.

'On the whole,' said Juana, 'I am quite prepared to see my—father.'

The door of the drawing-room burst open, and Bridget's head appeared.

'Miss Teresa, there's someone in the sheds,' she cried. 'I heard a noise like that of the Banshee of MacGillicuddy. Eh! Miss Juana, and is it yesilf I see?'

At the sight of the circus-girl Bridget wept, but she did not leave the vicinity of the door.

'Turn out every light,' said Richard.

No sooner had he said the word than he leapt up and extinguished the lamp which hung from the middle of the ceiling.

'Run, Mrs. Bridget,' he commanded, 'and put out the others.'

Bridget departed.

The other three went out into the porch, and at Richard's suggestion Juana led her mare away behind the house. They were obliged to leave the car where it stood, since it was impossible to move it without noise.

The house was now in darkness. Bridget had joined the rest in the porch. They stood braced, tense, silent, waiting—waiting for they knew not what.

Presently was heard the 'birr' of the electric motor-car from the direction of the outbuildings, and then the vehicle flashed down the boreen at fifteen or twenty miles an hour. Owing partly to the darkness and partly to the height of the glazed 'cab' of the machine, a contrivance designed by Mr. Craig himself, the driver of the car could not be recognised, but both Richard and Teresa thought that it could be no other than Raphael Craig, and, further, that he was alone. Just as the car passed Juana's mare whinnied, and there was an answering whinny from the orchard field where, as it afterwards appeared, Mr. Craig's two mares had been turned out to grass. But the car showed no inclination to halt.

'Sure the master will be after taking it away!' Bridget exclaimed.

'Taking what away, Bridget?' Juana asked.

'Micky's cor——'

'Silence, Bridget, you foolish creature!' Teresa stopped her. 'If you can't talk sense you must go and sit in the kitchen alone.'

This threat resulted in a very complete silence on the part of Bridget.

The car turned southwards down Watling Street.

'He is going to the chalk-pit,' said Richard quietly.

'Perhaps we had better follow discreetly and see what happens,' said Teresa.

'I was about to suggest that,' said Richard; 'but we ought not all to go.'

'And why not, Mr. Redgrave?' Bridget demanded, in alarm at the prospect of being left.

'Because—well, because we had better not,' said Richard. 'Four will make too heavy a load for this car.'

'Juana,' said Teresa, 'you will stay here with Bridget. Mr. Redgrave and myself will reconnoitre, find out what we can, and return to you with as little delay as possible.'

'Very well,' said Juana, while old Bridget sighed a sad resignation.

In half a minute they had started and were following the car down the road at a pace which would have been dangerous had not Watling Street been deserted at one o'clock in the morning. The moon still shone, but her light scarcely did more than disclose the sides of the road. The electric car was too far ahead to be discerned.

'Miss Craig,' said Richard, 'your suspicions of what may have happened are obviously more serious than you care to admit. We do not know the nature of the adventure upon which we have embarked. Let me beg you to be frank with me.

So far as your knowledge goes, has Mr. Craig committed any act, wittingly or unwittingly, which might bring him within the meshes of the law?'

'Do you mean, do I know whether he has killed Micky, the detective?'

'No,' said Richard sharply; 'I mean no such thing. Go back earlier than the last few days. Go back a few years, and consider. Mr. Craig told me last night that a relative had died and left him a hundred thousand pounds in silver.'

'Yes,' said Teresa; 'that was Great-uncle Andrew, the man who went to Mexico and then turned "queer." Father has often told me of him.'

'You believe that you once had a Great-uncle Andrew who left all this silver to your father?'

'Certainly. I remember father having all the papers and things to sign, and him fetching the money in casks on his car.'

'Fetching it from where?"

'Oh, I don't know. I forget. Some place near London.'

'What should you say if I told you that you never had a Great-uncle Andrew, or that if there was such a person, he never left your father any money?'

'But we went into mourning!" said Teresa naïvely.

'Possibly,' said Richard.

'Do you mean to say that poor father made it all up?'

'With the greatest respect for your father, Miss Craig, I suspect that that was the case. I do not know for certain, but I suspect. Have you, too, not had suspicions? Answer that candidly.'

Teresa hesitated.

'Yes,' she said in a low voice. 'But I swear to you that I believed my father.'

The car went through the tiny village of Chalk Hill, and their talk was suspended. Further up the road they could see the open gate which led by a broad field-path to the chalk-pit, the path along which Richard had seen the elephant dragging the other motor-car two evenings ago. Richard directed the car gently through the gate and then stopped; they dismounted, and crossed the great field on foot.

'If the matter of the silver was all fair and square,' said Richard, 'why did your father deal with the coin so mysteriously? How did he excuse himself to you when he asked your assistance?'

'He didn't excuse himself,' said Teresa stiffly. 'I acted as he told me. I was his daughter. It was not my place to put questions. Besides, I enjoyed the business. Remember, Mr. Redgrave, that I am not a middle-aged woman.'

As they got on to the highest part of the field they saw at the far end the dim shape of the electric car.

They crept cautiously towards it, and saw no sign of Raphael Craig. At length, avoiding the zigzag path that led down into the pit, they reached the point where the chalk had been cut precipitously away. Still moving with all possible discretion, Richard lay on his stomach and looked over. Twenty-five feet below he saw Raphael Craig, standing, apparently in an attitude of triumph, over the prone form of Micky, otherwise Nolan, the detective. A lantern held by Craig showed plainly the drawn and stiffened features of the man from Scotland Yard.

Before Richard could prevent her, Teresa had also looked over.

'God!' she cried softly. 'Is my father a——'

She stopped. The old man glanced mildly upwards.

Richard and Teresa with one accord ran along the edge of the pit, and then down the zigzag path till they stood facing Raphael Craig, the prone body of the detective between them.

'What is this?'' questioned the old man coldly. pushing back the gray hairs from his forehead, 'Spying again?'

He looked intently at Richard. He seemed to ignore the silent form on the ground.

'Father,' cried Teresa, 'if you have killed him, fly. Take the motor-car and get away as far as you can and as fast as you can. Mr. Redgrave and I——'

'Kill him!' Raphael Craig exclaimed. 'Why should I kill him? I found him lying here—here where I came to seek him. He must have fallen over this miniature precipice.'

'He isn't dead,' said Teresa eagerly; she had knelt beside the detective.

'I did not suppose that he was. But if he had been it would have been only a just punishment.'

'Had we not better carry him to the house, sir?" Richard suggested quietly.

'As you wish,' said Raphael. 'It appears that you have taken charge of our affairs.'

'Mr. Redgrave is here at my urgent request, father,' said Teresa.

'You!" Raphael gazed at her hard. 'You! Shall I curse you as I cursed your sister?"

Nevertheless, he helped Richard to carry the body of the detective up the path and into the field—a task of considerable difficulty. When they reached the electric car they put the lifeless organism into the back part of it.

'Take him,' said Mr. Craig to Richard succinctly —'take him off.'

'And you?" said Richard.

'I will follow.'

Richard and Teresa got into the electric car and moved off down the field. They spoke not a word. Arrived at the house, the detective was taken upstairs and put into a bed by the three women. The lamps had been re-lighted. The little man had regained consciousness, but he was too feeble to give any utterance to his thoughts.

He pointed weakly to his head, whereon his nurses found a lump, but no other sign of injury. They surmised that he was suffering from concussion of the brain, how caused they could only guess. He drank a little brandy-and-water, and lay extended on the bed as though unwilling almost to put himself to the exertion of breathing.

The noise of the Décauville sounded outside. Teresa sprang to the window.

'Here is father, Juana,' she said anxiously. 'If he should come upstairs——'

'Go down and stop him from coming upstairs. Bridget and I will attend to this poor fellow.'

Her voice was charged with sympathy as she glanced at the sufferer on the bed. The reference to himself caused the detective to open his eyes.

'I fell over the edge of the pit,' he murmured faintly. 'It was owing to the short grass being so slippery after the rain.' He had no Irish accent now.

Then he closed his eyes again.

Teresa gave a sigh of relief as she left the room. Her father, then, was not in thought a murderer.

As she entered the hall from the stairs Raphael Craig and Richard came in through the front-door. They had housed the two cars.

'Where is he?' asked Raphael of his daughter.

'In the back bedroom, father. He is not seriously hurt.'

'I will go up and have a look at him,' said Raphael, actuated apparently by mere idle curiosity.

'No, father, don't!' Teresa pleaded. 'Bridget is looking after him, and I believe he is just going to sleep.'

Raphael gave a gesture of assent.

'And now, sir,' he said to Richard, opening the drawing-room door, 'a word with you.'

The two men passed into the drawing-room. Raphael was closing the door when Teresa stepped forward.

'I have also a word to say, father,' she remarked firmly.

'Say it to me afterwards, then,' he replied briefly.

'No. It is a word that must be said now.'

The old man, smiling slightly and ironically, pulled the door open and allowed his daughter to enter the room.

Raphael Craig sat down on the Chesterfield sofa, but Richard and Teresa remained standing, Richard, for his part, determined that there should be no beating about the bush; and he had not the least intention of allowing the old man to put him in the wrong by asking difficult questions. So he began at once, fixing his eyes on a greenish-coloured newspaper that stuck out of Mr. Craig's right-hand pocket.

'Mr. Craig,' he said, 'let me cut a long story short. I came up here a few days ago to bring you a Williamson electric car. True, I was for the time being a genuine employé of the Williamson Company, but that was not my real business. I confess to you, Mr. Craig, that I am a private inquiry agent. It was in my professional capacity that I visited your house.'

'Ah!' said Mr. Craig. 'You were, then, after all, a spy? I had guessed correctly.'

'Spy?' Richard repeated calmly. 'Yes; it is an epithet that has been applied to me before.' He glanced at Teresa, who met his glance fairly. 'To continue,' he said: 'I have abandoned my inquiries. To be precise, I gave up my mission this morning; therefore, since I am here again, I am not here as a spy.'

'What led you to abandon your mission, Mr. Inquiry Agent?' asked Raphael, stroking his gray beard.

'I gave it up, Mr. Craig,' said Richard plumply, 'out of regard for your daughter.'

'Indeed!' Raphael remarked, with the frostiest politeness. 'So my daughter is fortunate enough to have won your regard?'

'If you care to put it so.'

'But,' said Mr. Craig, 'all this does not account for your presence here to-night, Mr. Inquiry Agent.'

'I am here now——' Richard began, and then stopped.

'Mr. Redgrave is here now,' Teresa said, at the same time seating herself, 'because I asked him to come.'

'When did you ask him, girl?'

'I went to London on the Décauville to Mr. Redgrave's office, and——'

'You went to London alone?'

The old man sprang up thunderously, and the newspaper fell out of his pocket. Richard quietly picked it up from the floor. It was that day's *Westminster Gazette*.

'Bridget went with me,' said Teresa, quailing before her father's outburst.

It was evident from both their respective demeanours that Mr. Craig's temper was not one of absolute serenity.

'Bridget!' sneered Raphael. 'You went down to London to ask Mr. Redgrave to come up to Hockliffe?'

'I went to ask him to abandon his inquiries.'

'But still, you brought him back with you?'

'Yes.'

'At one o'clock in the morning?'

'Yes. But, father——'

'Miss Craig was in a very awkward situation,' said Richard.

'I agree with you,' the old man interposed.

'And I was anxious to do anything in my power to help her.'

'And you helped her by visiting this house at one o'clock in the morning during my absence?'

'Father,' said Teresa pleadingly, 'can't you and I discuss that aspect of the question afterwards? What is it that you want to ask Mr. Redgrave?'

'My girl,' said Mr. Craig, 'we will, if you please, discuss it now. Mr. Redgrave is equally involved with yourself. Remember that it was you that insisted on joining this little conference. You insisted on coming into the room.' Then he turned to Redgrave. 'What was the exact nature of the difficult situation in which you say my daughter was placed?'

'I will tell you, father,' said Teresa, standing up. 'If you insist on Mr. Redgrave hearing it, he shall. I had reason to think that either you had killed Micky, or that Micky had killed you.'

'And which proposition did you favour?'

'I favoured,' said Teresa, with a coldness equalling her father's, 'I favoured the proposition that you had killed Micky. Bridget heard a revolver-shot in the night. I knew that you kept a revolver. Bridget had previously heard you and Micky at high words. This morning you had disappeared without warning me. Micky had also disappeared. Father, you were not treating me fairly.'

'You consider that before I leave my house I must give you "warning" like a servant, eh, Teresa? I wonder what Mr. Redgrave thinks of all this.'

'I do not see that it matters what Mr. Redgrave thinks,' said Teresa.

'It matters greatly,' the old man contradicted; 'and I will give you the reason.' He walked across the room very deliberately to the tall clock. 'Mr. Redgrave will be your husband, Teresa.'

'Father!'

Richard tried to think of something suitable to such an extraordinary occasion, but could not.

'You have hopelessly compromised yourself with him, and he shall marry you.'

'Never!' said Teresa, with every nerve tingling with a girl's pride. 'I will die first!'

'Very well,' said Mr. Craig, with frightful calmness, 'you will die, Teresa.'

His lips were white, and his eyes blazed as he opened the clock-case and took therefrom a revolver.

'Mr. Craig,' said Richard, 'may I beg you to remain calm?'

'I am entirely calm, sir. Teresa, you have never heard your mother's story. It is the remembrance of that story which makes me firm now. Some day you shall hear it. You may think me mad, but I am not so. You may think me of uncertain temper, mysterious, secretive, a bully, perhaps a criminal. Well, you must think those things; but when you know all, if ever you do know all, you will forgive all.' His voice softened a little, and then grew firm again. 'In the meantime, you shall marry Mr. Redgrave. You have visited his room at an unconscionable hour; he has visited this house at an hour still more unconscionable, and there is only one alternative to marriage. I am quite serious when I say that I would sooner see you dead than that you should remain single after this episode. I have seen what I have seen. I know your blood. I know what darkened my life, and darkened your mother's life, and finally killed her.'

'You threaten——' Teresa began.

'Stop, Teresa!' Richard exclaimed masterfully, and turning to Raphael Craig: 'Mr. Craig, nothing will suit me better. I have the honour to ask your daughter's hand.'

Teresa started violently.

'As Teresa's father,' said Craig solemnly, 'I give her to you. May she prove a worthy wife!'

'And you?' Richard questioned, gazing at Teresa.

'What a farce!' Teresa sobbed; but at the same moment, try how she might to prevent it, a smile lighted her tears, and her hand found Richard's hand.

Mr. Craig put the revolver back into the clock-case.

'I expect you know that we didn't yield to that tool of yours,' said Richard half playfully. 'I am truly fond of Teresa—that is the explanation. You wouldn't have used that revolver, though you are certainly in some ways a strange man.'

'As you are good enough to say, Redgrave, I am a strange man. I should have used the revolver.'

The way in which these words were uttered

created a profound impression on Richard. Releasing Teresa's hand, he began to consider what course he should now adopt in the joint interest of himself and of Teresa. He could not dismiss the suspicion that he had a madman to deal with.

'If I may,' said he to Mr. Craig, 'I should like a few words with Teresa outside. After that there are several things to be settled between you, sir, and me.'

Mr. Craig nodded.

'It is late,' he said.

'Yes,' said Richard, 'but such nights as this do not follow every day in the week.'

'Teresa!' the young lover exclaimed when they were in the hall, 'say you don't regret. I have loved you since the moment I saw you first.'

'I don't regret,' she said simply. 'Why should I?'

'Call me Dick,' he demanded.

'Dick.'

'And kiss me.'

She kissed him.

'Thanks,' he said in his curious, undisturbed way; 'that is indeed good. Now go to bed and rest. I will have a thorough explanation with your father at once. I am determined on that. We must know where we stand, you and I;' and without waiting for her to make any reply, he flung back into the drawing-room and slammed the door.

Raphael still sat on the Chesterfield, apparently lost in thought.

'Mr. Craig,' Richard began, 'I am now, for practical purposes, a member of your family. Your interests are, presumably, your daughter's interests, and your daughter's interests are certainly my interests; therefore——'

'Therefore?' repeated Mr. Craig imperturbably.

'Therefore,' said Richard, 'don't you think you had better let me into some of your secrets?'

'As, for example——'

'The secret, for example, of what has occurred between you and Micky, whose real name you have doubtless learnt since I left you on Saturday night last. I should tell you that I had ascertained the identity of that gentleman immediately upon the conclusion of my interview with you.'

'And I,' said Mr. Craig, 'ascertained it about twenty-four hours later. It was then that the revolver-shot occurred. The revolver-shot hurt no one and nothing except the piano.' Here Mr. Craig lifted up the embroidered damask cover of the piano, and showed splintered wood beneath. The perforation in the damask cover was scarcely noticeable. He continued: 'I was angry at the man's calm insolence when I taxed him with being a detective. I aimed to hit, but aimed badly. Having missed, I thought better of the idea of an immediate killing, and told him to go. He went.

I saw nothing of him again till I saw him lying senseless in the pit to-night; but I guessed that he was still prowling about.'

'Thanks,' said Richard.

'Thanks for what?' asked the old man.

'For your candour. I hope you will trust me and confide in me.' Richard was now trying to be extremely diplomatic. 'In spite of appearances, I still believe that you are an honourable man, engaged, however, in some scheme which may involve you in difficulties. Mr. Craig, let me beg you, most respectfully, to continue your frankness; you can lose nothing by it. I need not point out to you that you have been very fortunate to-night.'

'In what way?'

'In the fact that I happen to have fallen in love with Teresa, and was tempted beyond resistance by the opportunity offered by your amazing proposition. My love for Teresa has not, I hope, impaired my judgment, and my judgment infallibly tells me that you had a far more powerful reason than that of propriety for urging my engagement to your daughter. And, Mr. Craig, I venture to guess that your reason was that I knew too much of your affairs. You discerned the nature of my feelings towards your daughter, and you determined on a bold stroke. You are an incomparable actor.'

Mr. Craig slowly smiled; it was a smile of almost tragic amusement.

'Your insight does you credit, Redgrave,' he said at length. 'I admit that it was part of my wish to secure your silence, and perhaps your co-operation. Nevertheless, my chief reason for insisting on a betrothal was a regard for Teresa's future. There are pages in the history of my life that——' He stopped. 'We will not go into that,' he said shortly.

'As you please,' Richard assented. 'Perhaps, to change the subject, you will tell me your object in disappearing so completely to-day, to the grave alarm of my future wife?'

The youth's spectacles gleamed with good-humoured mischief.

'I had to perform a certain excursion,' said Raphael Craig.

'Now, why in the name of fortune, sir, don't you say at once that you went to London?'

'How do you know that I went to London?'

'By this paper.' Richard pointed to the *Westminster Gazette*, which lay on the floor. 'It is to-night's special edition. The *Westminster Gazette* is not on sale in Hockliffe.'

'Yes,' said the old man half dreamily, 'I went to London.'

'In order to close finally the estate of your uncle, who left you all that silver?'

The irony of Richard's tone was not lost on the old man.

'What do you mean, boy?"

'I said a few moments ago, sir, that you were

an incomparable actor. I alluded to our previous interview in this room. Most cheerfully I admit that Teresa's father imposed on me then to perfection. I believed you absolutely. Since then——'

'What?'

'Since then I have found out that you never had any uncle, and that, consequently, your uncle, being non-existent, could not have left you a hundred thousand pounds in silver coin.'

Raphael Craig took a long, deep breath.

'Yes,' he said, 'I lied to you. But it was a good lie—a lie which I have used so often during the last year or two that I had almost come to believe it truth. You are a clever fellow, Redgrave. How did you discover this?'

'To be precise,' said Richard, 'it was not I, but your precious Micky, who discovered it.'

'Then you are not so clever a fellow.'

'Clever enough, sir, to go straight to the point. And the point is, the point at which I have been gradually arriving since our talk began—how did you become possessed of that silver? I ask the question, and I demand an answer to it, as the affianced of your daughter.'

At this moment the lamp, short of oil, began to give a feeble and still feebler light. A slight smell of oil filled the room. Both men instinctively glanced up at the lamp.

'Redgrave, I may, at any rate, assure you that you are not about to marry a thief's daughter.'

'No, sir; probably not. But I may be about to marry the daughter of a man who in some other way has made an enemy of the law.'

'Listen,' said Raphael Craig, 'and believe that I am not acting now. Twenty years ago I formed a scheme, a life-plan. To the success of this scheme money was absolutely essential, money in large quantities. How was I to get it? I was in the service of a bank, and this fact was very helpful to the success of my scheme. I therefore did not wish to leave the bank. But a bank manager cannot make money. At least he cannot make much money. I needed a lot. I thought and thought, and at length I arrived at the solution of the problem. I began to *make* money.'

'But how?' asked Richard, not yet caring to seem to perceive the old man's meaning.

'I made it—made it steadily for nearly twenty years.'

'You coined it?'

'I coined it.'

'Then during the whole of this time you have been spreading bad money everywhere, and have never been found out?'

'I didn't make bad money, Redgrave. I made perfectly good money. I cheated no one. I merely sinned against the law. The price of silver, as you know, has been steadily decreasing for many years. The silver in a half-crown, as silver, is now worth little more than a shilling. A half-crown piece is only worth half-a-crown because we choose to call it so. Consult any book on coinage, and you will find that what I say is strictly true. What more easy, then, given the mechanical skill, which I possessed, than to make and utter genuine money at a substantial profit? I made a profit of fifty per cent. on my coinage, and no one on earth can distinguish my money from that of the Mint. It will stand any test.'

Richard did not conceal that he was impressed by the fine simplicity and effectiveness of Raphael's scheme.

'But,' the old man continued, 'I made money faster than I could get rid of it. It gradually accumulated. Then it was that I invented my Mexican uncle, so that I might deal with the coin more openly.'

'Yes?' said Richard.

'That is all,' said Raphael Craig.

'But the object of the scheme?' asked Richard. 'You said you needed all this money for a certain scheme.'

'Yes,' said the old man solemnly, 'and the scheme is approaching fruition. Yet a little time, and my task will be done.'

'It is well,' Richard put in, 'that your scheme is nearly completed, for the methods you have employed might even now be found out, and then good-bye to the scheme, whatever it is.'

Raphael Craig smiled.

'No, my friend,' he remarked composedly, 'nothing can upset it now. The last of my silver is disposed of—safely negotiated. Go into my sheds now, and you will discover—nothing. My machinery is destroyed; all evidence is annihilated. For twenty years I have been crossing an abyss by means of a tight-rope; at any moment I might have been precipitated into the gulf. But at last I am on firm ground once more. It is the Other, now, who will shortly be plunged into the abyss.'

'The Other!' Richard repeated, struck by the strange and mordant accent with which Raphael Craig had pronounced that word.

'The Other,' said the old man. 'His hour comes.'

'And who is he?' demanded Richard.

'That,' Raphael Craig said, 'you will never know until my deed is accomplished. The train is laid, the fuse is ignited. . . . I have only to wait.'

'Then you will tell me nothing more?' said Richard.

'Have I not interested you so far?' said the old man.

'Undoubtedly, but my curiosity is still not quite sated.'

'It occurs to me that your curiosity exceeds mine. By what right, young man, do you put all these questions? I have never sought to cross-examine you, as I might have done.'

'Under the circumstances,' said Richard, 'I think you have a perfect right to know, and certainly I have no objection to telling you. I came on behalf of the directors of the bank.'

'Which means Mr. Simon Lock,' said Raphael Craig.

'Which means Mr. Simon Lock,' Richard cheerfully admitted.

'Ah!'

'Then you decline to admit me further into your confidence?' Richard doggedly persisted.

'Redgrave,' said the old man, standing up, 'my scheme is my own. It is the most precious thing I have—the one thing that has kept me alive, given me vitality, vivacity, strength, hope. During all these years I have shared it with none. Shall I share it now? Shall I share it with a man young enough to be my son, a man who forced himself into my house, wormed himself into the secrets of my private life? I shall not. It is too sacred a thing. You do not know what my scheme means to me; you cannot guess all that is involved in it. I can conceive that you might even laugh at my scheme—you who do not yet know what life is and what life means.'

Raphael Craig resumed with dignity his seat on the sofa. Richard was impressed by this exhibition of profound feeling on the part of the old man. He was inclined to admit, privately, that perhaps the old man was right—perhaps he did not know what life was and what life meant; perhaps there were things in life deeper, more terrible, than he had ever suspected.

A silence fell upon the room. The old man seemed not inclined to break it; Richard, still under the hypnotism of the scene, would not speak. To relieve the intensity of the moment he quietly opened the *Westminster Gazette*. The lamp had sunk lower and lower, and it was with difficulty that he could read. His eye, however, chanced to fall on the financial page, and there, as the heading of a paragraph in the 'Notes,' he saw these words: 'LOCK RUMOURS.' He brought the page nearer to his face, and read: 'The rumours that the Lock group are in serious difficulties was again rife on 'Change to-day. Mr. Simon Lock, seen by one of our representatives, merely smiled when told of the prevalence of these sinister rumours. He gave our representative the somewhat cryptic answer that we should see what we should see. We do not doubt the truth of this remark. Dealing in the shares of the newly-floated "La Princesse" Gold Mining Company (Westralian) was very active this morning, but fell flat after lunch. The one-pound shares, which, after a sensational rise last week, fell on Thursday to a shade over par, are now at five and a half, with a distinct tendency to harden, in spite of the fact that the demand is slight.'

Richard looked up from the paper.

'I see,' he said, with interest, 'that it is not absolutely all plain sailing even with the great

Simon Lock. Did you read this paragraph here about him?'

'No,' murmured the old man. 'Read it to me.'

Richard did so in the rapidly-dying light.

'Very curious and interesting,' said Raphael Craig. 'I have sometimes permitted myself to wonder whether our respected chairman is, after all, the impregnable rock which he is usually taken for.'

At this moment the lamp went out, and the two men sat in absolute darkness.

The next ensuing phenomenon was the sound of an apparently heavy body falling down the stairs into the hall, and then a girl's terrified scream.

Richard sprang to the door, but a few moments elapsed before his fingers could find the handle. At length he opened the door. The lamp in the hall was still brightly burning. At the foot of the stairs, in an attitude of dismay, stood Juana.

There was a heavy and terrible sigh at Richard's elbow. He turned his head sharply. Raphael Craig stood behind him, his body swaying as though in a breeze.

'Juana!' he stammered out hoarsely, his eyes fixed on the trembling girl.

'Do not curse me again, father,' she cried, with a superb gesture; 'I have suffered enough.'

An oak chest stood to the left of the drawing-room door. Raphael Craig sank down upon it, as if exhausted by a sudden and frightful emotion.

'Go!' he said in a low voice.

But the girl came steadily downstairs towards him.

No one seemed to take any notice of the body of the detective.

CHAPTER XI

END OF THE NIGHT

THE body of the detective lay, by chance, lengthwise along the mat at the foot of the stairs. In order to reach the hall, therefore, Juana had no alternative but to step over the prone figure. This she did unhesitatingly, and then turned to Richard.

'Carry the poor fellow upstairs, will you?' she asked quietly. 'He is delirious. The room overhead.'

Richard obeyed. The small, light frame of the detective gave him no trouble. At the top of the stairs he met Mrs. Bridget hastening towards him.

'Holy Virgin!' she exclaimed. 'I did but run down by the backstairs to the kitchen and left the spalpeen with Miss Juana, and when I came back to them the room was as empty as my pocket.'

'He got a bit wild,' Richard explained. 'I suppose his head is affected. Miss Juana is talking with her father. Where is Miss Teresa?'

'Sure, she's gone out to the mares. They must have their water, if every soul of us was dying.'

Richard carefully laid Nolan on the bed in the room over the porch. By this time the sufferer had recovered consciousness. He murmured a few meaningless strings of words, then sighed.

'I will leave him with you,' said Richard.

'Not alone! If he begins to kick out——'

'He's quite quiet now,' said Richard, closing the door behind him.

Richard was extremely anxious to be present, as he had a sort of right to be, at the conversation between Raphael Craig and Juana. He descended the stairs with such an air of deliberation as he could assume, and stood hesitatingly at the foot. He felt like an interloper, an eavesdropper, one who is not wanted, but, indeed, there was no other place for him to put himself into, unless it might be the kitchen; for the drawing-room lamp was extinguished, and the lamp in the dining-room had not been lighted.

Juana had approached her father, who still sat on the oak chest. She bent slightly towards him, like a figure of retribution, or menace, or sinister prophecy. Richard noticed the little wisps of curls in the nape of her neck. She was still dressed in her riding-habit, but the lengthy skirt had been fastened up by means of a safety-pin. Richard could not be sure whether father or daughter had so much as observed his presence in the hall.

'I'll stay where I am,' he thought. 'I'm a

member of the family now, and it's my business to know all the family secrets.'

For at least thirty seconds Juana uttered no word. Then she said, in a low vibrating voice:

'Why do you tell me to go, father?'

'Did I not say to you last year,' the old man replied, 'that if you left me you must leave me for ever?'

'You abide by that?' the girl demanded.

'I abide by it,' said Raphael Craig.

Like a flash, Juana swept round and faced Richard, and he at once perceived that she had been aware of his presence.

'Mr. Redgrave,' she said, with head in air, and nostrils dilated, 'Teresa has just told me that at my father's—er—suggestion you and she have become engaged to be married.'

'That is so,' said Richard politely. 'May we hope for your congratulations?'

She ignored the remark.

'Do you know whom you are marrying?' she asked curtly.

'I am under the impression that I am about to marry the daughter of Mr. Raphael Craig, manager of the Kilburn branch of the British and Scottish Bank.'

'You are about to do nothing of the sort,' said Juana. 'Mr. Raphael Craig has no daughter. Teresa and myself, I may explain to you, are twin-sisters, though I have the misfortune to look much the older. We have always passed as the daughters

of Mr. Craig. We have always called him father.
Teresa still thinks him her father. It was only
recently that I discovered——'

'Juana,' the old man interrupted, 'have you,
too, got hold of the wild tale? It is astonishing
how long a falsehood, an idle rumour, will survive
and flourish.'

'There is no falsehood, no idle rumour,' said
Juana coldly; 'and I think it proper that Mr.
Redgrave should know all that I know.'

'It will make no difference whatever to me,'
said Richard, 'whose daughter Teresa may be.
It is herself, and not her ancestors, that I shall
have the honour of marrying.'

'Still,' said Juana, 'do you not think that you
ought to know Teresa's history?'

'Decidedly,' said Richard.

With an embittered glance at her father, Juana
resumed:

'Some time ago, Mr. Redgrave, a difficulty
between Mr. Craig and myself led to my leaving
this house. I was the merest girl, but I left. I
was too proud to stay. I had a mare of my own,
whom I had trained to do a number of tricks. I
could ride as well as most. Bosco's circus happened
to be in the neighbourhood. I conceived the wild
idea of applying for a situation in the circus. Only
a girl utterly inexperienced in life would have
dreamt of such a thing. The circus people had
me performing for them, and they engaged me.
On the whole I lived a not unhappy existence. I

tell you this only to account for my presence not long since in Limerick.'

'Limerick!' exclaimed Raphael Craig in alarm. 'You have been there?'

Juana continued calmly:

'The circus travelled in Ireland, and eventually came to Limerick. I knew that Limerick was my mother's home, and I began to make inquiries. I found out that my sister and I were born previous to Mr. Craig's marriage with my mother. She had been married before, or she had, at least, been through the ceremony of marriage with another man—a man unknown, who came suddenly into her life and as suddenly went out of it. You will gather, then, that Mr. Craig is not our father, and that he has no authority over us.'

'Redgrave,' muttered Raphael Craig, 'I tell you the poor girl is mad.'

Juana resumed quietly:

'I must inform you of another thing. While in Limerick and the district I met this Nolan, the detective. He had another name there. I know now, from what my sister has told me, that he must have been investigating the early history of my mother, and my real and false fathers, for some purpose of the police. But I judge him as I found him. He was very kind to me once, and I liked him. He was the personification of good-nature and good temper. When our ways parted he expressed the certain hope that we should meet again. We have met again, under circumstances·

extremely painful. He has not yet recognised me. You may ask, father,' she went on, turning to Raphael Craig, 'why I came back to your house to-day. There were two reasons. It is three months since I learnt about my parentage, and during the whole of that time I have been debating with myself whether or not to come and have it out with you. I inclined more and more to having a clear understanding, not only for my own sake, but for Teresa's. Then, the second reason, the circus folk had begun to talk. There were jealousies, of course; and the rumour that my birth was surrounded by doubtful mysteries somehow got afoot in the tents. I decided to leave. Here I am. I came prepared for peace; but you, father, have decided otherwise. I shall leave to-morrow morning. We have no claim on each other. Mr. Redgrave, that is all I have to say.'

She ceased.

Richard bowed, and looked expectantly towards the old man, but the old man said nothing.

'I have the right to ask you, sir,' said Richard, 'for your version of what Miss Juana has just told us.'

'We will talk of that to-morrow,' answered the old man testily. 'We will talk of that to-morrow.'

'It is already to-morrow,' said Juana scornfully.

There was a sudden tremendous racket overhead. A scream could be heard from Bridget, and a loud, confused chattering from Nolan. The latter rushed violently half-way downstairs, his eyes burning, Mrs. Bridget after him.

'I tell you I won't stay there!' he shouted. 'It's unlucky—that room where Featherstone slept the night before he killed himself! It's unlucky!'

The restless patient sank on the stairs, exhausted by the exertion. Before Richard could do anything, Mrs. Bridget, that gaunt and powerful creature, had picked up the little man, and by great effort carried him away again. The people downstairs saw no more of him. Mrs. Bridget had at last made up her mind to take him firmly in hand.

Richard was startled by a light touch on his shoulder, and he was still more startled when he caught the horror-struck face of Juana—the staring eyes, the drawn mouth.

'Tell me,' she said, her finger still on his shoulder —'tell me—I cannot trust him—has Mr. Featherstone committed suicide? Is he dead?'

'Yes,' said Richard, extremely mystified, but judging that simple candour would be the best course to adopt under the circumstances. 'There was an inquest. Didn't you see it in the papers?'

'Circus folk seldom trouble with newspapers,' she said. 'When was it?'

'About a month ago.'

'Poor fellow!'

Tears ran down her cheeks, and she spoke with an accent indescribably mournful.

'You knew him?' Richard suggested.

'I should have been his wife a year ago,' said Juana, 'had *he* not forbidden it.' Again she pointed to Raphael Craig. 'I never loved Mr. Featherstone, but I liked him. He was an honourable man—old enough to be my father, but an honourable man. He worshipped me. Why should I not have married him? It was the best chance I was ever likely to get, living the life we lived— solitary, utterly withdrawn from the world. Yes, I would have married him, and I would have made him a good wife. But *he* forbade. He gave no reason. I was so angry that I would have taken Mr. Featherstone despite him. But Mr. Featherstone had old-fashioned ideas. He thought it wrong to marry a girl without her father's consent. And so we parted. That, Mr. Redgrave, was the reason why I left the house of my so-called father. Scarcely a month ago Mr. Featherstone came to me again secretly, one night after the performance was over, and he again asked me to marry him, and said that he had decided to dispense with Mr. Craig's consent. He begged me to marry him. His love was as great as ever, but with me things had changed. I had almost ceased even to like Mr. Featherstone. I was free, independent, and almost happy in that wandering life. Besides, I—never mind that. I refused him as kindly as I could. It must have been immediately afterwards that the poor fellow committed suicide. And you'—she flashed a swift denunciatory glance on Raphael Craig—'are his murderer.'

The old man collected himself and stood up, his face calm, stately, livid.

'Daughter,' he said, 'daughter—for I shall still call you so, by the right of all that I have done for you—you have said a good deal in your anger that had been better left unsaid. But doubtless you have found sufficient justification for your wrath. You are severe in your judgments. In youth we judge; in age we are merciful. You think you have been hardly done to. Perhaps it is so; but not by me—rather by fate. Even now I could tell you such things as would bring you to your knees at my feet, but I refrain. Like you, I am proud. Some day you will know all the truth—the secret of my actions and the final goal of my desires. And I think that on that day you will bless me. No man ever had a more sacred, a holier aim, than that which has been the aim of my life. I thank God it is now all but achieved.'

He lighted one of the candles which always stood on the bookcase in the hall, and passed into the drawing-room, where he sat down, leaving the door ajar.

Richard crept towards the door and looked in. The old man sat motionless, absently holding the candle in his hand. The front-door opened from the outside, and Teresa ran into the house. She saw her father, and hastened, with a charming gesture, towards him.

'Old darling!' she exclaimed; 'why that sad face, and why that candle? What are you all doing? See!' she pulled back the shutters of the window. 'See! the sun has risen!'

So ended that long night.

CHAPTER XII

THE NAPOLEON

WE have now to watch another aspect of the great struggle which for so many years had been maturing in secrecy and darkness, and the true nature of which was hidden from all save one man.

It was seven o'clock in the morning, and in a vast bedroom of a house in Manchester Square a man lay with closed eyes. The house was one of those excessively plain dwellings of the very rich which are characteristic of the streets and squares of the West End of London. Its façade was relieved by no ornament. You saw merely a flat face of brick, with four rows of windows, getting smaller towards the roof, and a sombre green front-door in the middle of the lowest row. The house did not even seem large, but it was, in fact, extremely spacious, as anyone could see who put foot into the hall, where two footmen lounged from morn till night. The bedroom to which we have referred was on the first-floor. It occupied half the width of the house, and looked out on the square. Its three windows were made double, so that no sound from outside could penetrate that sacred apartment. Ventilation was contrived by means of two electric fans. The furniture consisted of the articles usual in an English bedroom, for the man in bed prided himself on being an Englishman who did not ape foreign ways. The said articles were, however, extraordinarily large, massive, and ornate. The pile of the immense carpet probably could not have been surpassed by any carpet in London. Across the foot of the carved oak bedstead was a broad sofa upholstered in softest silk.

An English bracket-clock on the mantelshelf intoned the hour of seven with English solemnity, and instantly afterwards an electric bell rang about six inches over the head of the occupant of the bed.

He opened his eyes wearily. He had not been asleep; indeed, he had spent most of the night in a futile wakefulness, which was a bad sign with a man who boasted that as a rule he could sleep at will, like Napoleon. Here was one detail out of many in which this man considered that he resembled Napoleon.

He groaned, pulled his gray moustache, stroked his chin, which bristled with the night's growth of beard, and ran his fingers through his gray hair. Then he touched an electric button. Within ten seconds a valet entered, bearing the morning papers—not merely a judicious selection of morn ing papers, but every morning paper published in London.

'Put them on the sofa, Jack.'

'Yes, sir.'

The man rose out of bed with a sudden jerk. At the same moment the valet, with a movement which would have done credit to a juggler, placed a pair of bath slippers on his master's feet, and with another movement of equal swiftness deposited a pair of six-pound dumb-bells in his hands.

The man performed six distinct exercises twelve times each, and then dropped the lumps of iron on the bed, whence the valet removed them.

'Seven-thirty,' said the man.

'Yes, sir,' said the valet, and disappeared.

The man sank languidly on to the sofa, and began, with the efficiency of a highly-practised reader, to skim the papers one after the other. He led off with the *Financial News*, proceeded to *The Times*, and took the rest anyhow. When he had finished, the papers lay in a tangled heap on the thick carpet. This man was pre-eminently tidy and orderly, yet few things delighted him more than, at intervals, to achieve a gigantic disorder. It was a little affectation which he permitted himself. Another little affectation was his manner of appearing always to be busy from the hour of opening his eyes to the hour of closing them. He was, in truth, a very busy man indeed;

but it pleased him to seem more deeply employed than he actually was. He had a telephone affixed to his bed-head, by means of which he could communicate with his private secretary's bedroom in the house, and also with his office in Cannon Street. This telephone tickled his fancy. He used it for the sake of using it; he enjoyed using it in the middle of the night. He went to it now, and rang imperiously. He did everything imperiously. There was a tinkling reply on the bell.

'Are you up, Oakley? Well, get up then. Go to Cannon Street, and bring the important letters. And tell——' He went off into a series of detailed instructions. 'And be back here at half-past eight.'

The clock struck half-past seven. The valet entered as silently as a nun, and the modern Napoleon passed into his marble bath-room. By this time everyone in the household—that household which revolved round the autocrat as the solar system revolves round the sun—knew that the master had awakened in a somewhat dangerous mood, and that squally weather might be expected. And they all, from the page-boy to the great Mr. Oakley, the private secretary, accepted this fact as further evidence that the master's career of prosperity had received a check.

At eight o'clock precisely the master took breakfast—an English breakfast: bacon, eggs, toast,

coffee, marmalade—in the breakfast-room, a room
of medium size opening off the library. He took it
in solitude, for he could not tolerate the presence of
servants so early in the morning, and he had neither
wife nor family. He poured out his own coffee
like one of his own clerks, and read his private
letters propped up one by one against the coffee-
pot, also like one of his own clerks. He looked
at his watch as he drank the last drop of coffee.
It was thirty-one minutes past eight. He walked
quickly into the library. If Oakley had not
been there Oakley would have caught it; but
Oakley happened to be there, calmly opening
envelopes with a small ivory paper-cutter. It was
mainly in virtue of his faculty of always 'being
there' that Oakley received a salary of six hundred
a year.

'Shall you go to Cannon Street this morning, sir?' asked Oakley, a middle-aged man
with the featureless face of a waiter in a large
restaurant.

'Why?'

'Sir Arthur Custer has telegraphed to know.'

'No.'

'I thought not, and have told him.'

'Umph!' said the master, nettled, but not daring
to say anything.

Like many a man equally powerful, this
Napoleon was in some ways in awe of his unexceptionable clerk. Oakley might easily get
another master, but it was doubtful whether

his employer could get another clerk equal to Oakley.

'A light post this morning, sir,' said Oakley.

'Umph!' said the master again. 'Take down this letter, and have it sent off instantly: "Richard Redgrave, Esq., 4, Adelphi Terrace. Dear Sir,—I shall be obliged if you can make it convenient to call on me this morning as early as possible at the above address. The bearer can bring you here in his cab.—Yours truly."'

The letter was written, signed, and despatched.

'Anything from Gaunt and Griffiths?' asked the Napoleon.

'Yes, sir.'

Oakley turned to a letter on large, thick, quarto paper. The stationery of this famous firm of stock-brokers—perhaps the largest firm, and certainly the firm with the cleanest record on the Exchange—was always of an impressive type.

'They say, "We are obliged by your favour of to-day's date. We can offer a limited number of La Princesse shares at twenty-five. We shall be glad to have your acceptance or refusal before noon to-morrow.—Your obedient servants, Gaunt and Griffiths."'

'Twenty-five!' exclaimed the other. 'They mean five. It's a clerical error.'

'The amount is written out in words.'

'It's a clerical error.'

'Doubtless, sir.'

Even now the Napoleon would not believe that misfortune, perhaps ruin, was at his door. He doggedly refused to face the fact. It seemed incredible, unthinkable, that anything could happen to him. So we all think until the crash comes. He plunged into the mass of general correspondence with a fine appearance of perfect calmness. But he could not deceive Mr. Oakley.

At five minutes past nine there was a careful tap at the door. The messenger had returned from Adelphi Terrace. Mr. Redgrave was not at his rooms. He had gone out on the previous evening, and had not come in again. The landlady knew not where he was.

'Send again at noon, Oakley,' said the Napoleon.

In another minute there was another tap at the door.

'Come in!'—angrily.

The footman announced that Sir Arthur Custer had called.

'D——n Sir Arthur Custer!' said the master of the house. 'Here, Oakley, get out of this! I must see him.'

Oakley got out, and Sir Arthur was ushered in. Sir Arthur looked at his host queerly, and then with much care shut the door.

'I say, Lock,' he said, putting his silk hat on the table, 'it seems to me we're in a devil of a hole.'

'Indeed!' said Simon Lock cautiously.

'Yes,' Sir Arthur insisted. 'Of course I'm sure that when you asked me to join you in this Princesse affair——'

'You will pardon me, Sir Arthur,' said Lock, stopping him very politely and formally, 'I did not ask you to join me. It was yourself who suggested that.'

'Ah, well!' said Sir Arthur, with a little less assurance, 'we won't quarrel about that. At any rate, I understood from you that we were in for a deuced good thing.'

'That is so,' Lock returned. 'By the way, sit down, Sir Arthur, and remain calm.'

'Am I not calm?' asked the member of Parliament, whose pomposity was unaccustomed to be trifled with.

'Certainly you are calm. I merely ask you to remain so. Now to come to the business in hand. I said, you remind me, that we were in for a good thing. So we were. But some secret force has been working against us. If I could unmask that secret force all would be well, for I could then bring pressure to bear that would effectually—— You understand?'

'No matter from what direction the force came?'

'No matter from what direction. And, Sir Arthur,' said Simon Lock impressively, 'I shall find it out.' He repeated the phrase still more impressively, 'I shall find it out. Simon Lock has never yet been defeated, and he will not be defeated now. I began life, Sir Arthur, on half-a-crown a week. There were conspiracies against me then, but I upset them. At the age of fifty-five, on a slightly larger scale'—he smiled—'I shall repeat the operations of my early youth.'

Simon Lock, like many self-made men, was extremely fond of referring to his early youth and the humbleness of his beginnings. He thought that it proved an absence of snobbery in his individuality.

'And in the meantime?'

'In the meantime, I frankly confess, Sir Arthur, we have sold more La Princesse shares than we can deliver. Nay, further, we have sold, I fear, more La Princesse shares than actually exist. We sold freely for the fall. I knew that the shares would fall soon after the flotation, and they did. But they have mysteriously risen again.'

'And are still rising,' Sir Arthur put in, nervously stroking his long, thin beard.

'Yes. We sold, I find, over two hundred thousand shares at three. They then fell, as you know, to about twenty-five shillings. Then they began to go up like a balloon. The market tightened like a drawn string. Sir Arthur, we were led into a trap. For once in a way some fellow has got the better of Simon Lock—temporarily, only temporarily. My brokers thought they were selling shares to the public in general, but they were selling to the agents of a single buyer. That is evident.'

'How do we stand now?'

'We have to deliver our shares in a week's time. We have some eighty thousand shares in hand, bought at various prices up to five pounds. On those eighty thousand we shall just about clear ourselves. That leaves us over a hundred and twenty thousand yet to buy.'

'At the best price we can obtain?'

'Yes.'

'And what is the best price to-day?'

'Well,' said Lock, looking Sir Arthur straight in the face, 'I have had shares offered to me this morning at twenty-five.'

Sir Arthur's reply was to rush to the sideboard and help himself to a glass of brandy. He was a timid creature, despite his appearance.

'And that figure means that we should lose the sum of twenty-two pounds on each share. Twenty-two times one hundred and twenty thousand, Sir Arthur, is two millions six hundred and forty thousand pounds. That would be the amount of our loss on the transaction.'

'But this is child's play, Lock.'

'Excuse me, it isn't,' said Simon Lock. 'It is men's play, and desperately serious.'

'I don't understand the methods of the Stock Exchange—never did,' said Sir Arthur Custer, M.P. 'I only came into the City because a lot of fellows like yourself asked me to. But

it seems to me the only thing to do is to cry
off.'

'Cry off?'

'Yes. Tell all these people to whom we have
contracted to sell Princesse shares that we simply
can't supply 'em, and tell 'em to do their worst.
Their worst won't be worse than a dead loss of
over two and a half millions.'

'My dear Sir Arthur,' said Simon Lock, 'there
is no crying off in the City. We have contracted
to deliver those shares, and we must deliver them,
or pay the price—commercial ruin.'

'The Stock Exchange,' Sir Arthur blustered, 'is
one of the most infamous institutions——'

'Yes,' Simon Lock cut him short, 'we know all
about that. The Stock Exchange is quite right
as long as we are making money; but when we
begin to lose it immediately becomes infamous.'

Sir Arthur made an obvious effort to pull himself together.

'What is your plan of campaign, Lock?' he asked.
'You must have some scheme in your head. What
is it? Don't trifle with me.'

'Well,' said Simon Lock, 'we have a week. That
is our principal asset. Seven precious days in
which to turn round. A hundred and sixty hours.
In that time——'

There was a knock at the door, and a page entered
with a telegram.

Simon Lock opened it hurriedly. The message
ran:

'Sorry must withdraw offer contained in our letter yesterday.   Princesse   shares   now   thirty-five.— GAUNT AND GRIFFITHS.'

The erstwhile Napoleon passed the orange-coloured paper to Sir Arthur Custer.

'No answer,' he said calmly to the page.

CHAPTER XIII

THE VASE

THE sensation of the next day's Stock Exchange was the unsuccessfulness of the attempts of Simon Lock's brokers—he employed several different firms—to buy La Princesse shares. It was not definitely stated who wanted these shares, but everyone seemed to be aware that Simon Lock was the man in the hole. The Exchange laughed quietly to itself; it did not dare to laugh aloud, for Simon Lock was still a person to be feared. Not a single share was to be obtained at any price; they had all been withdrawn from the market. In vain Simon Lock tried to discover the holders. The identity of the holders seemed to be wrapped in impenetrable mystery. He went to one man, a member of the Westralian market, who varied the excitements of the Exchange by the excitements of prodigious play at Monte Carlo, and took him out to lunch. The great Simon Lock actually took this man, a nonentity in the distinguished financial circles in which Simon moved, out to lunch at a famous and expensive restaurant, where those City men who want real turtle soup can always get it.

'My people sold you ten thousand Princesse shares the other day,' said Simon Lock ingratiatingly to this man.

'True,' said the man cautiously, 'at three.'

'Just so,' said Lock; 'and we have to deliver in a week.'

'In a week,' repeated the man absently.

'Well, look here,' said Simon Lock, making a sudden plunge, 'we don't want to deliver; it doesn't suit us. See?'

'You don't want to deliver? Why not?'

'Never mind why. The question is, what will you take to release us from the contract?'

'Nothing.

'You'll release us for nothing?'

'I mean I can't release you, Mr. Lock,' said the man with formal politeness. 'My clients have given me positive instructions.'

'Who are your clients?'

'That I am not at liberty to say.'

'Tell me who your clients are,' said Simon Lock, 'and I'll give you five thousand down.'

The man shook his head sadly. He would have liked that five thousand, but he dared not accept it.

'Are you acting for Gaunt and Griffiths?' asked Simon Lock.

'No,' said the man, glad to be able to give a positive answer.

'Waiter, the bill,' Simon Lock cried, and then gave a sigh.

The bill came to thirty shillings—thirty shillings wasted! He reflected that in a few weeks' time, unless something happened, he might be in serious need of that thirty shillings. Nevertheless, such is human nature, the idea of Simon Lock being hard up for thirty shillings was so amusing to him that he could not dismiss a smile. The other man wondered what evil that smile portended.

Simon Lock proceeded from the restaurant to the offices of Gaunt and Griffiths. He demanded to see Mr. Gaunt, the venerable head of the firm, and Mr. Gaunt kept him, Simon Lock, waiting ten minutes! Simon Lock had not suffered such an insult for years. At his name the most obdurate doors were accustomed to open instantly.

'Well, Mr. Gaunt,' he said, with an affectation of breezy familiarity, when at length he was admitted, 'I've just called about the matter of those Princesse shares. How many can you offer?'

'We can offer ten thousand, Mr. Lock.'

'At thirty-five?'

'At thirty-five.'

'That means three hundred and fifty thousand pounds for your holding?'

'Exactly.'

'Don't you wish you may get it, Mr. Gaunt? Eh! eh!'

He laughed gaily, but suddenly it occurred to him that his laugh sounded hollow and foolish, and he stopped.

'What do you mean?' asked Mr. Gaunt gravely.

'I mean,' said Simon Lock lamely, 'that the price is, of course, a fancy one. You know the market is a bit tight, and you're playing a game. You'll take less than thirty-five if you really want to sell.'

'Our firm is not in the habit of playing games, Mr. Lock. And, by the way, your last words bring us to the point. You say "if we really want to sell." The fact is, we don't want to sell. You will remember that it was you who came first to us to ask if we had any shares to offer. We made inquiries, and found some. Our clients——'

'Would you mind telling me,' Simon Lock interrupted, 'who your clients are?'

'It would be useless for you to approach them personally,' said Mr. Gaunt.

'I don't want to approach them personally. I shall not dream of such a breach of etiquette,' said Simon Lock, with an assumed fervour of righteousness. 'I merely wanted to know, out of curiosity.'

'I regret that I cannot satisfy your curiosity, Mr. Lock.'

'Then that is your last word, Mr. Gaunt—ten thousand at thirty-five?'

A boy entered with a telegram, which Mr. Gaunt perused slowly through his gold-rimmed spectacles.

'No,' said Mr. Gaunt; 'I regret to say—at

forty. I have just received further instructions
by telegraph.'

He waved the telegram in the air.

Simon Lock's face grew ugly, and he spoke with
ominous coldness.

'Someone seems disposed to make fun of me,
Mr. Gaunt,' he said. 'I don't know who it is, but
I shall find out; and when I do find out, there
will be trouble for that someone. I'll let this
cursed city know that Simon Lock is not to be
trifled with.'

'Good-day,' said Mr. Gaunt calmly.

Simon Lock went out furious. On the pavement
outside he met the office-boy who had brought
in the telegram to Mr. Gaunt.

'Where are you going to, my boy?" asked Simon
Lock kindly.

'To the post-office, sir,' said the boy.

'So am I. Now would you like to earn a couple
of sovereigns easily?' Simon Lock inquired.

'Yes, sir,' said the boy, and added, 'if it's all
square. Sovereigns ain't flying about, you know.

'It's all square. You won't do any harm to
anyone by earning it. All I want you to do is
to go into the post-office and say that on the last
telegram sent to your firm the name of the office
of despatch isn't stamped clearly. Ask them to
refer and tell you what it is. They know you, I
suppose?'

'Oh yes, sir.'

'Well, run along.'

The boy, dazzled by the glitter of sovereigns, went. Simon Lock waited for him outside the post-office.

'What's the answer?' he asked when the boy came out.

'They said I ought to have brought the form with me,' said the boy, 'but I talked to 'em like a father. I reckon I know how to manage them girls.'

'And what's the name of the place?'

'Hockliffe.'

'Here's your two sovereigns,' said Simon Lock gladly.

The lad capered down the street in the exuberance of joy.

Simon had learnt something. And yet, when he thought over what he had learnt, he seemed to think somehow that it was valueless to him. He had guessed all along who was at the bottom of the La Princesse business. His guess had been confirmed—that was all. He had threatened that, when he knew, he would do such and such dreadful things; but what could he, in fact, do? Should he send for Raphael Craig and threaten him? With what? It would be absurd to threaten with dismissal from a post worth at most a thousand a year a man who stood to gain hundreds of thousands from you. No; that manœuvre would not serve. At last he decided that he would pay a surprise visit of inspection to the Kilburn office of the British and Scottish Bank, and then act as circumstances dictated.

He jumped into a hansom.

'Kilburn,' he said shortly.

'What ho!' exclaimed the driver, not caring for such a long journey; 'Kilburn, eh? What's the matter with the Tuppenny Toob?'

However, Simon Lock insisted on being driven to Kilburn, and was duly driven thither, though at a pace which suited the horse better than it suited Simon Lock. The latter revenged himself —but not on the horse—by paying the precise legal fare.

He walked into the bank. No one knew him. His august presence caused no flutter of excitement. The cashier inquired briefly what he wanted.

'The manager,' said Simon Lock.

'Mr. Craig?'

'If you please.'

'Mr. Craig is taking his annual holiday.'

'Thanks,' said Simon Lock, grinding his teeth, and walked out. He had experienced exactly the same rebuff as Richard Redgrave a few days previously.

That evening, though he had several engagements, including one to dine at the house of a Marquis in Park Lane, Simon Lock dined at home in Manchester Square. The entire household trembled, for the formidable widower was obviously in a silent and bitter rage. He found the indefatigable Oakley in the library.

'Has that ass Custer been here again?' he asked.

'No, sir,' said Oakley; 'that ass Sir Arthur Custer has not been here within my knowledge.'

Many a clerk of Simon Lock's had suffered sudden dismissal for a far slighter peccadillo than this sally on the part of Mr. Oakley. The fact was, Simon Lock was too surprised at the pleasantry, coming as it did from a man who seldom joked, to take any practical notice of it. The two men— the clerk and the Napoleon of finance—glanced at each other.

'You are in a devilish merry humour to-night, Oakley!' exclaimed Simon Lock.

'It is my birthday, sir.'

'How old are you?'

'Between thirty and sixty, sir.'

'Listen,' said Lock; 'you shall come and dine with me. I never knew you in this mood before. I don't feel like laughing myself, and I may give you the sack before we get past the fish; but come if you like.'

'With pleasure, sir.'

So they dined together in the great dining-room of the mansion, with a footman apiece, and a butler behind the footmen. Mr. Oakley's mood was certainly singular to the last degree. Some people might have thought that his careless hilarity was due to the effects of intoxication, but this was not the case. And yet surely no one except a drunken man would have dared to behave to Simon Lock as he behaved. Mr. Oakley made deliberate fun

of his master before the three menials, and the
master never flinched nor jibbed. The fish was
safely passed without an explosion, and the joint,
the poultry, the sweets, and the priceless Cheshire
cheese followed without mishap. When the coffee
and cigars came round Simon Lock dismissed his
servants.

'Oakley,' he said, 'why are you going to give
me notice to leave?'

'I had no intention of leaving you, sir.'

'I could swear,' said Lock, 'that you had had
the offer of a better place, and were just amusing
yourself with me before giving notice. It would
be like you to do that, Oakley. You were always
a bit of a mystery. I suppose you have come
to the conclusion that Simon Lock's career is
over?'

'Nothing of the kind, sir. I have merely been
jolly because it is my birthday.'

'Well, Oakley, as it is your birthday, I don't
mind confessing to you that I am in something of
a hole.'

'Over the La Princesse shares?'

'Yes.'

'It is a pity,' said Oakley, 'that we have been
unable to lay our hands on Richard Redgrave.'

'You think, then, Oakley, that Redgrave, if we
could catch him and make him speak, might be
able to throw light on this little affair?'

'At any rate,' said Oakley, 'he might tell you
why he so suddenly threw up his job.'

'Yes, I would give something to get hold of Redgrave.'

'I felt that so strongly, sir, that I have myself been down to his place twice.'

'And have discovered nothing?'

'Nothing. But——'

'Well, what is it?'

'I was just thinking about the death of Featherstone. Featherstone lived in a couple of rooms in Blenheim Mansions, off the Edgware Road. Furnished rooms they were, let by a woman who has two flats on the same floor, and lets them out in small quantities to bachelors.'

'Yes?'

'I wanted a couple of rooms myself.'

'Have you not sufficient accommodation here?'

'I wanted, as I was saying, a couple of rooms myself, and I had a fancy to take the two rooms once occupied by the deceased Featherstone. It was a morbid fancy, perhaps. The landlady seemed to think so. Anyhow, I took them. I entered into possession this afternoon, and locked the door.'

'Did you expect to see his ghost? Featherstone killed himself at the bank, not in his rooms.'

'I am aware of it, sir,' said Oakley. 'I did not expect to see his ghost; I merely wanted to look round.'

'Look round for what?'

'For anything interesting that I might be able to see.'

'But surely the police had searched?'

'Yes, but they had found nothing. And I knew how anxious you were to find out anything that might be discovered about Featherstone's suicide.'

'Was that your reason for taking the rooms?' Simon Lock sneered.

'Why not?' said Oakley. 'Why should it not have been my reason? I have always been loyal to you, sir.'

'Well, well, did you find anything interesting, any trace of evidence that might clear up the mystery?'

'There was apparently nothing in the rooms except the ordinary furniture of an ordinary lodging. In the bedroom a bed, a dressing-table, a washstand, a small table, a small wardrobe, two chairs, a small carpet, a few framed prints, and some nails behind the door. Nothing that could be called evidence. In the sitting-room—rather more elaborately furnished—were a dining-table, six chairs, an easy-chair, a fire-screen, a large carpet, two footstools, a small sideboard, an old "Canterbury," a mirror, some oleographs framed in German gold, and a few vases on the mantelpiece. Here is one of the vases.'

Mr. Oakley jumped from the table and took from Simon Lock's own mantelpiece a small vase, whose intruding presence Simon Lock had not noticed there. Mr. Oakley handed it carefully to Mr. Lock.

'Do you notice anything peculiar about it?' he asked.

Simon Lock examined the vase attentively. It was in the shape of a cylinder, about seven inches high and three inches in diameter, and evidently a Staffordshire imitation of classic pottery. The ground-colour of the exterior was a brilliant red, and on this red were depicted several classic figures in white, with black outlines. Round the top edge the vase had been gilded. The interior surface of the vase was highly glazed.

'No,' said Simon Lock, 'I see nothing peculiar about it.'

'Neither did I at first, sir,' said Mr. Oakley; 'but see here.'

He wetted the end of his finger, and drew from the interior of the vase a roll of stiffish white writing-paper.

'That roll of paper,' he said, 'must have been dropped into the vase, whereupon it widened out till it filled the vase. The width of the paper happened to be exactly the height of the vase, and so the paper looked exactly like the internal surface of the vase. The resemblance would deceive almost anyone. I thought, as you did, that the vase was absolutely empty, but it was not.'

'And the paper?' asked Simon Lock.

'The paper,' said Mr. Oakley, holding the strangely-hidden document in his hand, 'is double, as you see. On the inside it is filled with small writing, very small writing, and the signature is that of Featherstone. I have read it, and I have brought it here as a surprise for you—I hope a pleasant surprise. Hence what you were pleased to call my devilish merry humour.'

'Give it me,' said Simon Lock briefly.

His voice trembled.

'Here it is, sir.'

Simon Lock took the paper, and began to read with difficulty.

'Turn another light on,' he said, and Mr. Oakley obeyed.

CHAPTER XIV

FEATHERSTONE'S RECITAL

AND this is what Mr. Simon Lock read, while Mr. Oakley watched his master's face. The caligraphy of the document was miraculously neat and small, and the thing had all the appearance of a declaration formally made:

'Statement of me, Robert John Dalrymple Featherstone, made on the day before my death. (Here followed the date.)

'This statement is intended to be perfectly plain and simple. I put down facts as they occur to me in the most straightforward possible way. I have never before in my life undertaken any sort of literary composition, beyond letters to acquaintances. My parents dying when I was a boy, and me being an only child, I have had no relatives; nor have I ever had an intimate friend. I do not know why I am at the trouble to write out this statement now. I only know that I am compelled to make it by an instinct, or an impulse, which overpowers my ordinary commonsense. It cannot be a matter of any importance that the world should understand the circumstances under which

I am led to commit suicide. The world will
not care. And, on the other hand, this statement may work harm, or at least annoyance,
to one whom I love. Nevertheless I must write
it. Everyone, perhaps, who commits suicide
feels the tremendous desire to explain to the
world the reasons of his act—that act for which
there is no remedy, that act which he knows, if
he is a Christian, must involve him in eternal
remorse.

'As I write I have a sort of feeling that what I
put down may be printed in the newspapers. This
feeling causes me to want to write unnaturally,
in a strained and showy measure. I shall try to
avoid this. All my life I have lived quiet and
retired. This was not because I was modest. I
am not more modest than other mediocre men. It
was because I was shy and awkward and reserved
by nature in the presence of others. When I am
alone I feel bumptuous, audacious; I feel like a
popular actor.

'But let me begin.

'My age is fifty-six. For thirty years I have
been in the service of the British and Scottish
Banking Corporation, Limited. For eight years
before that I was in the service of a small private
bank in Northamptonshire. I have always served
the British and Scottish faithfully, to the best of
my ability. Yet after thirty years I was only a
cashier in a suburban branch with a salary of
two hundred a year—such an income as many a

more fortunate man spends on cigars and neckties.
I do not, however, blame anyone for this. I do
not blame myself. I realise clearly that I am a
very mediocre man, and deserved nothing better.
I never had any talent for banking. I never had
any talent for anything. I became a bank clerk
through the persuasion and influence of a distant
uncle. I agreed with him that it was an honourable and dignified vocation. It has suited me. I
got used to the official duties. I soon learnt how
to live within my income. I had no vicious
tastes—no tastes of any sort. I had no social
gifts. I merely did my work conscientiously.
My evenings I spent reading the papers and
periodicals and smoking. I have smoked two
ounces of Old Judge per week regularly for five-
and-twenty years. I have never smoked before
lunch except during my annual fortnight at the
seaside. Every morning at breakfast I have read
the *Standard*. My political opinions have never
varied.

'Thus my life has been one of absolute sameness.
There was no joy in it except the satisfaction of
regular habits, and there was no sorrow, until last
year but one (May 28th), when Miss Juana Craig
walked into the office at Kilburn.

'She said, "Is my father in his office?"'

'I did not know her, had never seen her before,
but I guessed at once that she was the daughter
of Mr. Raphael Craig, the manager of our branch.
I say she said, "Is my father in his office?" Nothing

beyond those words, and yet they had the same effect upon me as if they had been the most magnificent piece of oratory. I was literally struck dumb with emotion. There was something peculiar in her rich voice that overcame me. She was obliged to repeat the question.

'At last I said, "Miss Craig, I presume. No; Mr. Craig is not in, but he will be in shortly."

'I stammered this as though I had been repeating a badly-learnt lesson.

'She said, "Then I will wait in his room, if I may."

'The way she said those last three words, "if I may," made me feel dizzy. There was a sort of appeal in them. Of course I knew it was only politeness—formal politeness—yet I was deeply touched by it. And I felt ashamed that this beautiful girl should, in a way, have to beg a favour from old me.

'I said, "With pleasure." And then I took her into Mr. Craig's room, and she sat down, and said what wet weather we were having, and I tried to talk to her. But she was too beautiful. I could not help thinking all the time that my hair was gray, and my moustache part gray and part sandy, and that I had my office coat on, with paper shields over my wrist-bands, and that I was only five feet two inches in height. At last I came out of the room, and as I did so all the clerks looked at me, laughing, and I blushed violently. I do not remember ever blushing before.

'One clerk said jokingly, "Hello, Feather (they call me Feather), what ha' you been up to in there?"

'If I had been a bigger man I would have knocked him down.

'I had never had anything to do with women, except, in a purely business way, with our lady customers. Our lady customers all liked having their cheques cashed, etc., by me, because I was always so strictly polite to them. But, strange to say, I could not be polite to Miss Craig, though never before had I wanted so badly to be polite to any woman.

'After that day Miss Craig seemed to call every day, or nearly every day, for her father, just after closing time in the afternoon. She was on a motor-car, and they went off together up towards Edgware, Mr. Craig having a house in the country near Dunstable. Sometimes I came out on to the pavement to see them off. Once or twice I waved good-bye to them, and once I actually kissed my hand to Miss Juana. It was a very daring thing to do, and after I had done it I wished I had not done it, but I could not help doing it. She did not take offence, and the next day she was more charming than ever. She is the sweetest, most womanly creature that God ever made. My wonder is that the other clerks did not seem to see this. They never went further than to say that she was a pretty girl. I despised them. I despise them now more than ever.

'One Friday afternoon Mr. Craig said, "Feather-stone, have you anything particular to do this week-end?" I said that I had not. He said, "Well, will you come up with us to-morrow, and spend the week-end with us?"

'Before I could answer anything Miss Juana said, "Yes, do, Mr. Featherstone, there's a dear man. We should love to have you."

'The charming and adorable creature conde-scended to joke. I said, "I gladly accept your very kind invitation."

'So I went up and stayed at their house till the Monday morning. Miss Juana drove down on the motor-car, me sitting by her side, and Mr. Craig behind. It was very enjoyable.

'Mr. Craig himself was very polite to me during my visit, and so was Miss Teresa, Miss Juana's sister. Miss Teresa drove us back to London on the Monday morning. And for this I was sorry; not that I have a word to say against Miss Teresa, who is a pretty enough girl, and amiable. Just before we started on the journey to London Mr. Craig put a small but heavy portmanteau under the back seat of the motor-car. I asked him what that was, merely from idle curiosity, and he said, "Money, my lad." The two ladies were not about. I laughed, thinking he was joking. But that day he called me into his private room and said, in a very ordinary tone of voice, "Featherstone, here is fifty pounds in new silver. Pay it into my ac-count." "Yes, sir," I said, not thinking. It was the luncheon hour, and nearly all the clerks were out. I casually examined the silver. Of course I can distinguish a bad coin in a moment, almost by instinct. I seem to be mysteriously warned of the approach of a bad coin. But this money was all right. The next morning Miss Juana called in, and she and I had a chat. I liked her more and more. And, either I was an insufferably conceited ass, or she liked me. I knew there was more than thirty years' difference between us. But I said to myself, "Pooh! what is thirty years? A man is as young as he feels." I knew that I had only an income of two hundred a year, which might rise to two hundred and twenty-five or two hundred and fifty; but I said to myself that thousands of people married happily on less than that. I felt that it was impudent on my part to aspire to the hand of this angel; but I also said to myself that it was always impudence that succeeded.

'Anyhow, I was madly and deeply in love, I, bank cashier, aged fifty odd.

'Two hours after Miss Juana had called Mr. Craig called me into his room and said again in a very ordinary tone of voice: "Featherstone, here is another fifty pounds in silver. Pay it into my private account." As before, the money lay in piles on his desk. "Yes, sir," I said. I thought it very strange, but my mind was preoccupied with Miss Juana, and he was Miss Juana's father, so I said nothing else. Again, most of the other clerks were out when I filled up the slip and put the cash into the drawers. All that day I thought of Miss Juana. Let me say now that I am convinced she had no part in the plot, for it was a plot, which Mr. Craig laid against me.

'At the end of that week Mr. Craig had paid over two hundred pounds' worth of new silver into his private account, and these payments continued. In a fortnight I was asked down to the Craig's country house again. I cannot describe my courtship of Miss Juana. I find my statement is getting too long. But in any event I could not describe it. It was the most precious, the only precious fragment of my life. The only drawback to my timid happiness was Mr. Craig's attitude to me—a sort of insinuating attitude, quite at variance with the usual style of this powerfully-minded and very reticent man. The payments of new silver continued. In a business of the magnitude of our Kilburn branch the silver was, of course, distributed in the ordinary routine of affairs without special notice being taken of it.

'One day I proposed to Miss Juana. It was a terrible moment for me. To this hour I do not know how I dared to do it. To my inconceivable astonishment and joy Miss Juana said: "You honour me, Mr. Featherstone. I am a poor girl. My father is not rich. I do not love you, but I like you, and I esteem you. I accept your hand."

'Later I said to Mr. Craig: "Mr. Craig, I have asked your daughter Juana to be my wife, and she has done me the honour to consent. Do you also consent?"

'He said in reply: "My dear Featherstone, you will pardon me, but, of course, I know the amount of your salary. Have you any other resources?" I said that I had none.

'The interview grew strangely complex. I see now that he handled me with consummate skill and adroitness. It came to this. He said: "Assist me in a scheme of mine which is approaching completion, and when it is complete I will give you twenty thousand pounds. But you will be bound to secrecy."

'I said to him: "Is your scheme in any way contrary to the law?"

'He said: "Frankly, it is. But, Featherstone, you are in love, and there is no crime in my scheme."

'I admit that Mr. Craig's offer of twenty thousand pounds dazzled me at first, especially as I began instantly to perceive that my life's happiness would depend on my acceptance of it. You may ask what right a man aged fifty odd has to talk of a life's happiness—a man who probably has not more than ten years to live. Let me suggest that it is impossible for any man, however old, not to believe that he will survive for an indefinitely long period, unless he be actually on his death-bed.

'Moreover, I was profoundly in love. I loved with the intense and restrained passion of which only a middle-aged man in love for the first time is capable. No young man, with the facile ardours of youth, could appreciate my feelings. Be that as it may—and I have no wish at this solemn hour to attempt to excuse myself— my demeanour certainly gave Mr. Craig the impression that I had no objection to becoming his confederate. His face showed that he was pleased—that a weight had been lifted from his mind.

'He said: "Give me your oath that you will disclose nothing of what I am about to tell you."

'I said: "But suppose I do not see my way——"

'He interrupted me very grimly: "What does that matter? Anyhow, I presume you can see your way to hold your tongue?"

'So, not without qualms, I gave him an oath of secrecy. He then told me that he had been coining silver for many years—that his object had been to coin a hundred thousand pounds' worth, and that he was then at the end of his long task.

'I said: "But you just now told me that you had not involved yourself in any crime; surely to utter false money is a crime?"

'He said with sudden anger: "It is not false money: it is perfectly good money. It is exactly the silver produced by the Mint, and neither you nor anyone could tell the difference."

'He then explained to me how it was profitable for him, owing to the very low price of silver, to make real money, good in every respect. He finished by saying that no one was robbed by his device.

'I said: "Excuse me, but the Government is robbed, and, since the Government represents the public, the public is robbed. You are robbing the public. Besides, coining is a crime."

'He burst out: "Only in the eyes of the law. It is not a real crime."

'I said, as quietly as I could: "That may be; real or unreal, it is a crime."

'He went on, apparently not noticing my observation: "Anyhow, I find it necessary to put this money into circulation at a far quicker rate than I have previously achieved. The years are slipping by. I have by me vast accumulations of silver money, and I must negotiate them. I will tell you my object, Featherstone: it is to take a just revenge upon a scoundrel who, more than twenty years ago—before her birth— cast a shadow—a terrible shadow—over the life of the girl whom you love. Will not that move you?"

'I exclaimed: "Juana?"

'He said: "Yes, Juana and her sister and their poor mother. I have lived till now only to carry out that scheme—only to see this man at my feet ruined and begging for a mercy which I shall not vouchsafe."

'I own that I was moved to sympathy by the fearful earnestness of Mr. Craig. I asked him who the man was.

'He replied: "That I will not tell you, nor will I tell you his sin, nor the precise nature of my revenge, until you agree to join me. Surely you, as the professed lover of Juana, will not hesitate for a moment?"

'But I did hesitate.

'I said: "First, let me ask you one or two questions."

'He said coldly and bitterly: "Ask."

'So I asked: "You want me to help you in passing this coin which has not come from the Royal Mint?"

'He replied with eagerness: "Yes. I want one or two accounts opened at other banks, and certain operations put into action with financiers and specie dealers. Also, with your help, I can do a lot at our own bank."

'I said: "It seems to me you have already done something there."

'He laughed, and outlined to me the various means, all very ingenious, by which he had already disposed of a lot of silver.

'I said: "Another question: Am I to understand that if I decline to join you you will withhold your consent to my marriage with your daughter?"

'He answered: "If now, at this stage, you decline to join me, I would see both you and Juana dead before I allowed you to marry."

'His manner was ferocious. I could see that he was absolutely absorbed—that his whole moral being was cankered by this life-long idea of a mysterious revenge. And though I did not allow him to guess the fact, I was annoyed at his attempt to intimidate me. I am not to be intimidated.

'I said: "I will think it over, and give you my answer shortly."

'I saw Juana privately, told her that her father had not given me a definite answer, and returned to London in order that I might think the matter over with the more calmness. In the same house with that angelic presence it was impossible for me to think at all. I deem it right to state that I believed—and still believe—that Mr. Craig was telling me the truth, and that he was of sound mind. I truly believed—and still believe—that some man, the object of Mr. Craig's hate, had deeply wronged Juana, her sister and her mother, and that Mr. Craig was animated in all that he did by a lofty conception of human justice. I guessed, further, that there was probably no means by which Mr. Craig could bring this man, whoever he might be, before the tribunals of the law (how many crimes slip through the wide meshes of the law!), and that therefore he had no alternative but a private vengeance. The idea of vengeance on behalf of Juana—that beloved being—appealed strongly to my deepest feelings.

'Nevertheless, on mature consideration, I felt that I could not become a party to Mr. Craig's scheme. I have always tried to live an honest life, and I have never accepted the sophism that the end justifies the means. In three days I returned to the house near Dunstable and told Mr. Craig my decision. He was enraged.

'He said: "Then you prefer to give up Juana?"

'I said: "Do you think you are acting fairly in insisting that no man shall be Juana's husband unless he consents to commit a crime against the law?"

'He said: "Bosh!"

'Before such an argument I was dumb. I saw more and more clearly that Mr. Craig was what is called a monomaniac, and a very determined and obdurate one.

'After further and useless words, I left him and sought Juana.

'I said to her: "Miss Juana, your father forbids us to marry."

'She replied in a strange tone: "My father is a harsh man, Robert. He can be very cruel. Although I feel that he loves Teresa and myself passionately, you can have no idea of the life we live here. Sometimes it is terrible. Teresa is my father's favourite, and I—I sometimes hate him. I hate him now. Perhaps because I cannot comprehend him. Robert, I will marry you without his consent."

'I cannot describe my emotions at that moment. Her use of my Christian name thrilled me through and through. There was something in the tone of her voice which caused strange and exquisite vibrations in me. I thank God now that I had strength to behave as an English gentleman should behave.

'I said: "Miss Juana, your kindness overwhelms me. But I should be unworthy of your love if I took advantage of it. I am an old-fashioned man, with old-fashioned views, and I could not marry a lady in the face of her parent's opposition."

'Without a word, she ran out of the house. I saw that she was crying. A few minutes afterwards I saw her galloping wildly down the road on her strawberry-roan mare. She was the most magnificent and superb horsewoman I have ever set eyes on.

'The incident, as the phrase goes, was closed. I had enjoyed the acquaintance of Miss Juana for nearly twelve months. I enjoyed it no longer. The relations between Mr. Craig and myself resumed their old formality. He was nothing but the bank manager; I was nothing but the cashier. The pity was that I was bound to secrecy as regards his scheme; and I saw that his scheme was maturing. Without the slightest scruple, he made use of me to aid in disposing of his silver through the bank.

He could depend on my honour, though my honour made a criminal of me. Things got worse and worse. His methods grew bolder and bolder. A year passed. One day he told another clerk in the office that a great-uncle had died and left him a hundred thousand pounds in new silver. He turned to me, who happened to be close by.

'"A strange fellow! I have mentioned his peculiarities to you before now, have I not, Featherstone?"

'Scarcely knowing what I said, I answered, "Yes."

'I was thus by an audacious stroke made a party to his dodge for explaining away the extraordinary prevalence of new silver. Previously to this I had noticed that he was drawing large cheques in favour of a firm of stockbrokers.

'At length I could stand it no more. I went into his private room and said: "Mr. Craig, either you must cease your illegal proceedings, or you must release me from my oath of secrecy."

'He said flatly: "I shall do neither."

'Of course I could see that my request was foolish. He had me between his thumb and finger.

'I then said: "Very well, Mr. Craig, there is one alternative left to me—I resign my position in the bank. You force me to do this."

'He said: "As you wish."

'He was relentless. So I was cast on the world, at my age. I had no hope of obtaining another situation. But what else could I do? By remaining in the service of the bank, and allowing Mr. Craig to make it the channel for disposing of false money, I was betraying my trust to the bank. The truth was I ought to have done a year before what I did then.

'My savings amounted to about a hundred pounds.

'Soon after this final step I discovered, to my equal grief and astonishment, that Miss Juana had left her father's house—doubtless he had practically driven her forth—and was earning her living in a travelling circus. I ascertained where the circus was, and I had an interview with Miss Juana one night after the performance. Miss Juana was in her circus-dress, a curiously showy riding-habit, and she had paint on her dear face. The interview was inexpressibly painful to me. I cannot narrate it in full.

'I said: "Miss Juana, marry me. I implore you! Never mind your father's consent. Anything to save you from this. I implore you to marry me! I love you more than ever."

'I did not tell her that I had no means of livelihood now. I had absolutely forgotten the fact.

'She replied: "Why, Mr. Featherstone, I am getting an honest living."

'I said again: "Marry me."

'I could not argue.

'She said: "A year ago I would have married you. I liked you. But I cannot marry you now."

'I asked madly: "Why?"

'She replied: "Things have happened in the meantime."

'I returned to London last night and bought a revolver. It is my intention to kill myself in Mr. Craig's own room while he is out at lunch. This seems to me proper, but I may be mad. Who knows? My brain may be unhinged. As for my oath of secrecy, Raphael Craig cannot demand secrecy from a dead man. If this document leads to his punishment, let it. I care not. And Juana, as she says herself, is getting an honest living. She is independent of her terrible father.

'It is half-past one o'clock in the morning. In twelve hours I shall be in the beyond. I will place this statement in a vase on the mantelpiece. Let who will find it.

'Given under my dying hand,

'ROBERT J. DALRYMPLE FEATHERSTONE.'

When Simon Lock had finished the perusal of this document he passed his hand before his eyes. The dead man's handwriting, although perfectly clear, was so fine that even the delicate shades of Simon Lock's electric chandelier had not been able to prevent the august financier from feeling the effects of the strain; but the condition of his eyes was a trifle. He experienced a solid and satisfying joy—such joy as he had not felt for a very long time.

'You have read it?' he questioned Oakley.

'I took that liberty, sir,' said Oakley, who was now the old Oakley again—formal, dry, submissive.

'And what did you think of it, Oakley?'

'I thought, sir, that it might prove useful to you.'

'Did you assume that I was the unnamed man against whom this wonderful Raphael Craig is directing what he calls his vengeance?'

'Yes, sir.'

'Ah!' breathed Simon Lock. 'I've just got this in time.'

'You think that you have got it in time, sir?'

'Yes, my young friend. It is a nice question whether it constitutes legal evidence, but anyhow, it constitutes a lever which I think I can use pretty effectively upon Mr. Craig.'

'Then you deem it valuable, sir?'

'Yes,' said Simon Lock.

'What do you think it is worth to you, sir?'

Oakley looked peculiarly at his master, who paused.

'Well, Oakley,' he said at length, 'since you put it in that way, it is worth, we'll say, a hundred pounds to me. I'll draw you a cheque. It will pay the expenses of your summer holiday.'

'Thank you, sir,' said Oakley impassively. 'May I just glance at the document again, sir? There was one point——'

Simon Lock handed him the dead man's message. Oakley took it, folded it carefully, and placed it in his pocket.

'What the devil are you doing?' Simon Lock demanded angrily.

'I was venturing to think, sir, that, after all, the document belonged to me by right of discovery. And since I have the misfortune to differ from you as to its monetary value——'

Simon Lock jumped up, and then he looked rather cautiously at Mr. Oakley's somewhat muscular frame.

'Look here——' Simon Lock began imperatively.

'In my hip-pocket I have a revolver, Mr. Lock,' said Mr. Oakley. 'Force, therefore, would be a mistake.'

'I see,' said Simon Lock. 'Well, what do you think the thing is worth?'

'Ten thousand pounds,' said Mr. Oakley imperturbably. 'I will hand it over to you in exchange for a promissory note for that amount payable at three months.'

There was a long pause. Simon Lock had the precious gift of knowing when he was beaten.

'I accept,' he said.

'Thank you; here is the document,' said Oakley when he had received the promissory note.

After Simon Lock had transferred the paper to his own pocket he remarked:

'Oakley, the position which you occupy here is quite beneath your high capabilities. I dismiss you. I will write you out a cheque for a month's wages. Leave the house within an hour.'

'With pleasure, sir,' said Mr. Oakley, exactly as he had accepted the invitation to dinner.

CHAPTER XV

ARRIVAL OF SIMON

A T Queen's Farm, Hockliffe, the excitations of the terrible evening on which Juana faced her father, and on which Richard and Teresa were betrothed, seemed to have exhausted the actors in those trying scenes. Only Teresa herself maintained her spirits through a night of sleeplessness, and Teresa's eyes disclosed a simple and profound happiness of the soul, which proved how well the forced engagement with Richard suited her inclinations. As for Richard, he, too, was happy in the betrothal, but his experience of the world—a thousandfold greater than Teresa's—was responsible for forebodings that filled him with apprehension. He could not but feel that disaster—perhaps immediate disaster—waited upon the schemes of Raphael Craig, those schemes of whose success the old man was so proudly confident. Richard guessed, naturally, that Raphael Craig was waging war on Simon Lock, and his common-sense predicted with assurance that in this struggle of the weak against the strong, the strong would crush and the weak would be crushed. The exact nature of Raphael Craig's plan, of which Richard was still in ignorance, seemed to the young man to be a matter of comparative unimportance. He perceived, at any rate, that the campaign was a financial one. That was enough; in the realm of finance Simon Lock had long been peerless, and though, as the newspaper hinted, Simon was temporarily at a disadvantage, it was absurd to pretend for an instant that Raphael Craig, undistinguished, even unknown, could win.

So ran the course of Richard's thoughts as he lay resting during the early hours of the morning on the Chesterfield in the drawing-room. Raphael Craig had retired to his room. Teresa had also retired. Juana and Bridget were attending on the stricken detective. Each had expressed her intention of sitting up all night. Whenever Richard's somewhat somnolent meditations turned in the direction of the detective he could not help thinking that here, in this sick man, helpless, hurt, delirious, was the instrument of Simon Lock's ultimate success. Nolan knew, or Nolan shrewdly surmised now, that Raphael Craig had grossly outraged the Coinage Acts. Nolan had doubtless collected a sufficient body of evidence at least to secure a committal for trial, and so it was an indubitable fact to be faced that, immediately Nolan recovered, or partially recovered, the forces of the law would be set in motion against Craig—against Craig, the father of his betrothed. Then—Queen's Farm would doubtless explode like a bomb!

But was Raphael Craig the father of his betrothed? Had Juana lied on the previous night, or had the old man lied? Here were questions which Richard preferred to shirk rather than to answer.

A much more important question was, what would Raphael Craig be likely to do in regard to Nolan? As things stood, Nolan was at his mercy—helpless in his house. Certainly Craig would by this time have arrived at the conclusion that instantly Nolan was enabled to leave the house his own ruin would occur. Richard did not believe that Craig's scheme could possibly succeed after Craig was clapped in prison as a coiner. He, indeed, suspected that Craig had only made this boast in order to dispel any suspicions which Richard might entertain as to the bodily safety of Nolan within the precincts of Queen's Farm.

Yet it came to that: Richard was not without fear that the old man might attempt to murder Nolan. Nolan dead, and his body disposed of, Craig was safe. It was a frightful thought, but Raphael Craig's demeanour whenever he referred to his life-long scheme of vengeance gave at least some excuse for it.

At eight o'clock there was a tap at the drawing-room door. Richard jumped up and came out of the room. Bridget stood before him.

'Miss Teresa up?' he asked.

'No,' said the housekeeper, 'and not likely to be yet, the darling! I came to give ye a hint, Mr. Redgrave, that ye might do worse than seek a breakfast down in the village, at the White Horse.'

'How's the patient?' he asked.

'Micky, ye mean? Better—though the spalpeen doesn't deserve God's goodness nor Miss Juana's loving care.'

'Mr. Craig up?' he asked further.

'No,' said Bridget.

'Yes,' said Richard, 'I'll go down to the village, and come back again in a couple of hours.'

He passed quietly out of the house. He had, however, not the slightest intention of going down to the village. Determined to ignore the fact that he had been caught as a spy once, and the risk that he might be caught again, he turned to the left as soon as he was out of the garden and crept under the garden wall up to the sheds, which he cautiously entered. Safely within the range of buildings, he soon found an outlook therefrom which commanded a view of the house—a vantage-point whence he could see without being seen.

Nothing unusual occurred. Indeed, save that Bridget came forth to attend to the mares, having doubtless been instructed to do so by Teresa, nothing occurred at all till a little after nine o'clock. Then Mr. Craig issued quickly out of the house, went along the boreen, and down towards the village. At a discreet distance Richard followed him, for he deemed it his bounden duty to keep an eye on Raphael Craig until Nolan, the detective, should have departed from the house. It was not pleasant for him to think of his prospective father-in-law as a potential murderer, but he had no alternative

save to face the possibility.   It is a full mile from
Queen's Farm to Hockliffe village.   Mr. Craig,
however, walked quickly, and the distance was
soon accomplished.   The old man went into the
general store, which is also the post office—a tiny
place crammed with the produce of the East and
of the West.   After a moment's hesitation, Richard
also walked towards the post-office.   When he
reached it, Mr. Craig was in the act of paying for a
telegram.

'Hullo!   Good morning,' said Raphael Craig
blithely.   'What are you doing here?'

'I came for some stamps,' Richard answered.

'Hum!   They said you'd gone down to the village
for breakfast.   What with one thing and another,
our household arrangements are somewhat upset,
I'm afraid.   Ta-ta!'

Raphael Craig left the shop, apparently quite
incurious as to Richard's doings or plans for the
day.   Richard was decidedly reassured by the man's
demeanour.   He seemed as sane, as calm, as collected as a bank manager could be.   And yet—last
night!

Richard breakfasted at the hostelry of the White
Horse, and then walked slowly back to Queen's
Farm.   As he approached the house he met Raphael
Craig again going down to the village.   Four
times that day the old man went down himself
to the village post-office to despatch telegrams,
and he openly stated that he was going to despatch
telegrams.

Teresa was in the orchard, and Richard went to her. He said that he did not see how he could stay longer in the house, that he ought to return to London, and yet that he scarcely cared to leave.

To his surprise, Teresa appeared agitated and distressed at the mere idea of his leaving.

'Don't go at present,' she urged him. 'Stay at least another twenty-four hours. Just think how I am fixed. That man ill and delirious—by the way, Juana won't leave his side—and father and Juana not on speaking terms. There is no knowing what may happen. We needn't pretend to each other, Dick, that there isn't something very peculiar and mysterious about father. I dare say you know more than I do, and I shan't ask questions. I don't want to know, Dick, so long as you're here. But do stay a bit. Stay till something turns up.'

'Till something turns up?' He repeated her phrase. 'What do you mean?'

'I don't know,' she said simply; 'but stay.'

He kissed her.

That night Richard was provided with a bed, but he found himself unable to sleep on it. About the middle of the night—or so it seemed to him—there was a rap on his door.

'Mr. Redgrave.'

The voice was Juana's.

'Yes,' he answered. 'Anything the matter?'

'Can you come and speak to Mr. Nolan? He

wants to speak to you, and nothing else will satisfy him.'

Richard rose and dressed, and came out on the landing, where a lamp was burning. Juana, fully dressed, her eyes ringed with fatigue, stood waiting for him. She beckoned him down the side-passage, and he entered the room occupied by the sick man.

'Shut the door,' the sick man commanded in a febrile voice.

As though it had been previously arranged between them, Juana kept out of the room. Richard and the detective were alone together.

'You're looking better,' Richard said.

'Don't talk so loud,' said Nolan. 'That old scoundrel sleeps next door. Yes, I'm better,' he went on rather wearily, shifting the position of a pillow, 'thanks to nursing. I wish to say something to you. You know a good deal about my business up here. You've been on the same business yourself. Well, look here: if any questions are asked, I don't want you to know anything about what I've done or what I've found out.'

'Whatever do you mean?' Richard asked.

'Oh dear!' the other said pettishly: 'can't you understand? I mean down at Scotland Yard. If any of 'em should come to you, you know, say nothing. Fact is, I'm going to let the old man off, if I can—I'm bound to let him off. It's all got to be hushed up, if Mr. Nolan, Esquire, can manage it.'

'Why?' asked Richard calmly.

'Why did you chuck the job up?' returned Nolan. 'Can't I follow your example?'

'Do you mean that you—er—Miss Juana?'

'Precisely,' said Nolan. 'I met her down at Limerick months ago—long before the death of old Featherstone—when I was engaged on inquiries about old Craig's antecedents, to try if I couldn't throw any light on the matter of his treasure of new silver, which has interested the police for a year past. I met her. I hadn't the least notion that she was his daughter. I was afraid that I should never see her again. And then, when I woke up in the cursed little room here and found her bending over me—by Heaven, it was too much! For the time, I do believe, it made me worse. She has told me a lot to-day. I haven't been delirious since early this morning. Oh yes, Redgrave, I've got to chuck it. I wouldn't harm that woman, or anything that belonged to her— not to be Chief of Police in Paris! You and I must put our heads together and concoct a tale that will satisfy the people in London.'

The door opened and Juana entered with a firm step.

'Time's up,' she said, looking at the man in bed. 'I gave you five minutes, and you've had ten. Good-night, Mr. Redgrave, and thanks.'

Here indeed was spirited nursing.

Richard retired to his own room, intending to think things over, but instead of thinking, for some reason or other, he slept heavily till nine o'clock. Then he dressed and descended, and, seeing no one about, went into the garden. Almost at the same moment a light trap drove up to the garden-gate. Telling the driver not to wait, a man got down from the vehicle. It was Mr. Simon Lock.

'Ah! Mr. Redgrave,' said Simon Lock, 'you seem to be at home here. Can you tell me if Mr. Craig is at home?'

CHAPTER XVI

THE INTERVIEW

AT the same moment as Simon Lock spoke a window opened in the upper story of Queen's Farm, and Raphael Craig showed his head. Raphael Craig was fully dressed, and his face had the freshness of morning. Richard looked apprehensively from one to the other of these old men and old enemies, expecting from either or both an outburst of wrath—such a terrible outburst as twenty years might have prepared; but nothing of the kind happened.

'Good-morning, Mr. Lock,' said Raphael Craig blandly.

Simon Lock, equally with Richard, was astonished by the mildness of this greeting.

'Good-day to you,' said Simon Lock. 'You do not seem surprised to see me,' he added.

'Not in the least,' said Craig. 'On the contrary, I was expecting you.'

Simon Lock started.

'Ah!' was all he said.

'Excuse me one instant,' said Craig. 'I will be down immediately to welcome you to my house. You will, I trust, take breakfast with us. And you, too, Redgrave, will breakfast with us. Let me beg you not to run away as you did yesterday morning.'

The bank manager had positively turned courtier!

On his way down he intercepted Mrs. Bridget between the dining-room and the kitchen, and told her to have breakfast ready for five within half an hour.

'But——' began Mrs. Bridget, raising her bony hands.

'For five,' repeated Raphael Craig, 'in half an hour.'

Then he went forward, and invited Simon Lock to enter, and led him to the drawing-room, and Richard also. His attitude towards his guests, though a shade formal, was irreproachably hospitable. Anyone could see that Simon Lock felt himself at a disadvantage. The great and desperate financier had anticipated a reception utterly different; this suavity and benignity did not fit in with the plan of campaign which he had schemed out, and he was nonplussed.

Once he did manage to put in:

'I called to see you, Craig——'

'After breakfast, I pray,' the other cut him short.

A gong rang. Raphael Craig rose and opened the drawing-room door, and the three men passed into the dining-room. Coffee, bacon and eggs were on the table. The two girls—Teresa in a light summer frock and Juana still in her dark habit—stood by the mantelpiece. They were evidently in a state of great curiosity as to the stranger, the rumour of whose advent had reached them through Mrs. Bridget. Juana was, beyond question, perturbed. The fact was that at Teresa's instigation she had meant that morning to approach her father amicably, and was fearful of the up-shot. Raphael Craig, however, cut short her suspense. He kissed both girls on the forehead, and then said:

'Mr. Lock, let me introduce my daughter Juana, my daughter Teresa. My dears, this is Mr. Simon Lock, who has run down to see me on a matter of business, and will do us the honour of break-fasting with us.'

The meal, despite the ordinances of its service, had the deadly and tremendous formality of a state dinner at Buckingham Palace. Conversation led judicially by the host himself, was kept up without a break, but Simon Lock distinctly proved that the social arts were not his forte. The girls talked timidly, like school misses on their best behaviour, while Richard's pose and Richard's words were governed by more than his charac-teristic caution. Only Raphael Craig seemed at ease, and the old man appeared to take a ferocious but restrained delight in the unnatural atmosphere which he had created. It was as if he saw written on every face the expectation of some dreadful sequel, and rejoiced in those signs of fear and dread. His eyes said: 'Yes, I can see that you are all desperately uncomfortable. It is well. You are afraid of something happening, and you shall not be disappointed.'

'Now, girls,' he said lightly, after the meal was finished, 'go and amuse yourselves, and don't forget your poor patient upstairs.'

'You have someone ill in the house?' Simon Lock ventured.

'Yes,' said Craig; 'a fool of a Scotland Yard detective who got himself into trouble up here by ferreting about.'

Simon Lock turned pale.

'He was nearly killed,' Raphael Craig went on. 'We are nursing him back to life.' The old man laughed. 'And now for our business,' he said, and turned to Richard. 'I will see Mr. Lock in the drawing-room, and I shall ask you, Mr. Redgrave, to be present at our interview.'

'Is that necessary?' asked Simon Lock pompously.

'I have omitted to tell you,' said Raphael Craig, 'that Mr. Richard Redgrave is my prospective son-in-law, engaged to my daughter Teresa. I have no secrets from him.'

Simon Lock bowed. They returned to the drawing-room, and at a sign from Raphael Craig Richard closed the door.

'Now, Mr. Lock,' said Raphael Craig when they were seated, 'what can I do for you?'

'You said from your bedroom window that you were expecting me,' Simon Lock replied. 'Therefore you are probably aware of the nature of my business, since I have given you no warning of my arrival.'

Mr. Lock's face disclosed the fact that he had summoned all his faculties—and he was a man of many faculties—to the task that lay before him. Various things had irked and annoyed him that morning, but in order to retain the mien of diplomacy he was compelled to seem to ignore them. There could be no doubt, for example, that he bitterly resented the presence of Richard at this interview, but what could he do save swallow the affront? The whole situation was a humiliating one for Simon Lock, who was much more accustomed to dictate terms than to have terms dictated to him. Still, it was to his credit as a man of nerve and a man of resource that he was able to adapt himself to unusual circumstances. He had a triple feat to perform—to keep his dignity, to be diplomatic, and to be firm. He had come with a precise end in view, and he was willing to sacrifice everything to that end. Behold him, therefore, in the drawing-room at Queen's Farm—him, the demigod of the City, trying to show a pleasant and yet a formidable face under extraordinary trials.

'It is true,' said Raphael Craig, 'that I expected you. But it was my instinct more than anything else that led me to expect you. You come, I presume, about the shares of La Princesse Mine.'

'Exactly,' said Simon Lock.

'You have contracted to sell more of these shares than you can supply, and the price has risen?'

'Exactly,' said Simon Lock, smiling cautiously.

Raphael Craig was, so far, courtesy itself.

'And you wish to get the bargain cancelled?'

'I am prepared to pay for the accommodation.'

'And to get the bargain cancelled,' Craig pursued, 'you come to me.'

'I come to you,' repeated Simon Lock.

'Yet you have no direct knowledge that I had any influence over these shares.'

'No direct knowledge,' said Lock; 'but an indirect knowledge. Perhaps,' he added in a peculiar tone, 'I know more than you guess.'

'As for example?'

'Perhaps I could answer the question, which certainly demands an answer, how you, a mere manager of a branch of our bank, in receipt of a not excessive salary, found the money to become a power on the Westralian market. As the chairman of the directors of the bank I have, I think, Mr. Craig, the right to put that question.'

'You have first to prove that I indeed am a power on the Westralian market.'

'The proof of that is in the mere fact that I— I—am here at the present moment.'

Raphael Craig smiled.

'You are correct,' he said. 'That fact is a proof in itself. I admit that I am a power. To save unnecessary words, I frankly admit that I hold La Princesse Mine in the hollow of my hand. You have come to the proper person, Mr. Lock. We meet at last. And am I to understand that one object of your visit here is to discover how I became possessed of the means which a manipulator of markets must possess?'

'I confess I should like to know from your own lips.'

'Well, Mr. Lock, I shall not tell you. It is no business of yours. The sole fact that concerns you is that I am in a position to control this particular market, not how I arrived at that position.'

Raphael Craig's tone had suddenly become inimical, provocative, almost insolent.

Simon Lock coughed. The moment had come. He said:

'On the night before his decease the late Mr. Featherstone, whose death we all lament, wrote out a sort of confession——'

'You are mistaken,' said Raphael Craig, with absolute imperturbability; 'it was on the last night but one before his death. After writing it out, he changed his mind about killing himself instantly. He came up here to see me instead. He told me he had put everything on paper. He made an urgent request, a very urgent request, to me to reconsider a certain decision of mine. I declined to reconsider it. On the other hand, I thoughtfully offered him a bed. He accepted it, left the next morning, and killed himself. I merely mention these circumstances for the sake of historical exactitude. I suppose you have somehow got hold of Featherstone's document.'

At this point Richard rose and walked to the window. The frosty coldness, the cynical carelessness of Raphael Craig's manner made him feel almost ill. He was amazed at this revelation of the depth of the old man's purpose to achieve his design at no matter what cost.

'I have got hold of it—somehow,' said Simon Lock. 'You may judge what I think of its value when I tell you that I paid ten thousand pounds for it.'

'Hum!' murmured Craig. 'What surprises me is that the police did not get hold of it long ago. They must be very careless searchers. My opinion of Scotland Yard is going down rapidly.' He paused, and then continued: 'It was indiscreet of you, Mr. Lock, to pay ten thousand pounds for that document. It is quite useless to you.'

'I fear you cannot be aware what is in it,' said Simon Lock. 'It is indisputable evidence that during many years past you have been in the habit of coining large quantities of silver money.'

'What of that?'

'It means penal servitude for you, Mr. Craig, if I give it up to the police. But I trust you will not compel me to such an extreme course.'

'How can I persuade you to have mercy on me?" laughed Raphael Craig.

The other evidently did not appreciate the full extent of the old man's sarcasm.

'It will not be difficult,' said Simon Lock, 'provided you are reasonable. I will tell you without any circumlocution what my terms are.' Simon was feeling firm ground under his feet at last, as he thought. 'What my terms are.' He repeated the phrase, which seemed to give him satisfaction. 'You must instruct your agents to agree to a cancellation of the contracts to sell La Princesse shares. They must let go.'

'As those contracts stand, Mr. Lock, how much do you reckon you would lose on them?'

'I cannot say,' said Lock stiffly.

'I will tell you,' said Raphael Craig. 'You would lose something between two and a half and three millions of money. What you ask is that I should make you a present of this trifling sum.'

'In return I will give you Featherstone's document.'

'Nothing else? Nothing in solid cash?'

Simon Lock reflected.

'Yes,' he said, 'I will give you a hundred thousand in cash.'

'Make it a quarter of a million,' Raphael Craig affected to plead.

'I will make it a quarter of a million,' said Simon Lock, 'though I am condoning a felony. I will give you the document and a quarter of a million in exchange for a cancellation of all La Princesse contracts. That is a clear and businesslike offer.'

'It is,' said Craig. 'And I refuse it.'

'You want more? I decline to give it.'

'I don't want more. If you offered me ten millions I wouldn't accept it.'

'You prefer to go to prison? You prefer that I should give the document to the police?'

'I care not,' said Craig. 'I shall be perfectly content to end my days in prison. I have ruined you, Simon Lock.' He jumped up, and almost shouted, 'I have ruined you, Simon Lock, and I can die happy—whether in prison or out of it makes no matter. In four days hence the contracts must be fulfilled—you must deliver the shares, or you are a ruined man. And you cannot deliver the shares. I have seen to that. Let happen what may, the contracts are in safe hands. You will have noticed that my name does not appear

H

on them, and you are ruined. You are ruined, Simon, you are ruined—unless I choose to be merciful.'

He spoke the last words in low, deliberate tones, quite different from the rest of the speech, and this change evidently puzzled Simon Lock, who was now undecided whether still to maintain a peaceful attitude or to threaten and bluster.

Raphael Craig went on, looking at Richard: 'These great financiers, Redgrave—you see they are not so great after all. The genius of Simon Lock in juggling with other people's money is supposed to be transcendent, yet how easily I have juggled with his! It is not more than three months ago that I first saw my opportunity of working on a big scale. I obtained information about the probable tactics of the people in charge of Princesse shares, and I took my measures accordingly. By the way, it is surprising the number of people in the City who were delighted to assist me in ruining Simon Lock. The most staid persons seemed to take a fiendish glee in it.'

Simon Lock smiled rather grimly, and Raphael Craig pursued his way:

'I knew that the great Lock group were selling Princesse shares for the fall. It was very silly of them, though, to sell more than they could deliver, especially as there doesn't happen to have been a fall.'

'I am sure,' said Simon Lock, 'that you won't mind telling me who disclosed the nature of our operations in the matter of the Princesse shares.'

'With the greatest pleasure in the world,' said Raphael Craig. 'It was one of your own intimate gang—your private secretary, Oakley. I bought him, body and soul, for a thousand pounds.'

'And he sold you to me for ten thousand,' murmured Simon Lock, half to himself. 'I am well rid of him. And now'—he turned to Craig, and put some firmness in his voice—'do, please, come to some arrangement.'

'Arrangement!' exclaimed Raphael. 'A good joke! Certainly we will come to some arrangement. But first I must tell Redgrave, who has a right to know, the history of the girl he is about to marry. I will tell him in your presence, and when I make any error of fact you can correct me. Many years ago, Richard, I was engaged to a beautiful girl, a native of Limerick. She was an orphan, and had lived with friends until she became a school-teacher, when she lived by herself. She had some aristocratic Spanish blood in her veins through her mother's father, who had married her grandmother in Buenos Aires. I met her in Limerick when I was a clerk in the bank there. I fell in love with her. I asked her to be my wife, and she consented. We were to be married as soon as my salary had sufficiently increased. I then had an offer to a situation in the British and Scottish, just starting on its successful career, and I removed to London. We arranged that I should save every possible penny, and that we should get married in about two years' time. It was from motives of economy that I allowed a whole year to pass without revisiting Limerick. I continually received letters from my fiancée, and though their tone was never excessively warm, it was always tender, and it satisfied me. As for me, I was passionately in love. I had never seen such an adorable creature as my betrothed—her name was Juana—and I have never since seen her equal. For me she was, and always will be, the world's jewel. . . . Well, a change came over the scene. I noticed something in her letters—something which I could not define. Then, after an interval of silence, came a letter saying she could not marry me. I got leave of absence—not without a great deal of difficulty—and hastened over to Limerick. Juana had left Limerick. I found her at length in a remote mountain village, and I drew from her her story. It was a shocking one. A man—a stranger from London—who must have been a highly plausible person in those days, whatever he is now—had dazzled her by his professions of admiration and love. He was a rich man even then, and he made her a brilliant offer of marriage. The poor girl was carried off her feet. Unduly urged, and her mind poisoned by his lies concerning myself, her faith in me shaken by the stoppage for some weeks of my letters, she consented to marry this man. She married him. They lived together for a

brief period. And all this time she had not
courage to write and confess to me the truth.
Then the man left her, and coolly informed her
that the marriage was a bogus marriage from
beginning to end—that he was, in fact, already
married. He said he wished to have nothing more
to do with her, and gave her a bank-note for a
thousand pounds to solace her wounded feelings,
which bank-note she flung into the fire. You
may ask why this man was not prosecuted for
bigamy. I will tell you. The matter was kept
quiet in order to spare the feelings of my poor
deluded Juana. Think what the trial would have
meant to her. I myself arranged with the priest
and one or two other officials that the whole
thing should be buried in oblivion. I had reserved
my own punishment for the villain who thus
escaped the law. To proceed, Juana had two
children—twins. They were named Juana and
Teresa. Shortly after their birth their mother
died. But before she died—on her death-bed—I
married her. I had begged to do so before, but
she had declined. I swore to her that I would
regard Juana and Teresa as my own children, but
of my intended vengeance against her murderer
I said nothing. Hers was a gentle heart, and she
might have put me on my oath to abandon vengeance. From the day of her death I lived for
nothing save the punishment of a villain. It was
my one thought. I subordinated everything to it.
It made my temper uncertain; it involved me in

endless difficulties; it estranged me from my dear
one's elder daughter, and often I felt that I was
harsh to Teresa, my favourite and the last-born.
But I could not do otherwise. I was a monomaniac. I dreamt only of the moment, when I
should see my enemy at my feet, begging for
mercy. That moment has come. He is here.
Watch him. He could only be wounded in one
place—his pocket. His pocket is the heel of this
noble Achilles, and it is his pocket that my sword
has pierced.'

With outstretched finger Raphael Craig pointed
with passionate scorn at the figure of Simon
Lock.

'Beg for my mercy,' Craig commanded.

And to Richard's amazement Simon Lock
answered:

'I entreat your mercy, Craig.'

'That is well. I am satisfied,' said Craig. 'They
say that revenge turns to ashes in the mouth. I
don't think it does.'

'Mr. Craig,' said Lock suavely to Richard, 'has
given a highly-coloured account of a somewhat
ordinary affair. But to appease him I do certainly
ask his mercy. I do admit that he has the upper
hand.'

'And I will see you eternally damned, Simon
Lock,' said Raphael Craig, 'before I grant
you an ounce of mercy! There is no mercy for
such as you, who are never merciful yourselves.
I only wanted to hear you beg, that was all.

I hadn't the slightest intention of letting you off.'

Simon Lock got up.

'It is as well,' he said, 'that this farce should end. In asking your mercy I was only using a form of words in order to pacify you. I recognised that you were suffering, as you yourself have admitted, from a sort of mania, and I took what I thought was the easiest course with you. As to the past, we will not go into that. Your version of it is ridiculously overstated. I shall now leave. In twenty-four hours you will be in prison. You say that the fact of your being in prison will not affect the Princesse contracts. I think it will. I think that when I inform the Stock Exchange Committee that the real mover of those contracts is awaiting his trial as a coiner, the Committee will do something drastic. I might have told you this before, but I wished, if possible, to arrive at an amicable settlement. In offering you two hundred and fifty thousand pounds I fancy I was meeting you more than half-way. Good-day, Mr. Craig; good-day, Mr. Redgrave. And, Mr. Redgrave, have a care how you mix yourself up with this Craig, and, above all, do not take for gospel everything that he says as to my past history.'

Simon Lock made his exit from the room with immense dignity.

'He is bluffing,' said Raphael Craig. 'He is at the end of his tether, and he knows it; but he has bluffed it out very well.' The old man smiled happily. 'You are still prepared to marry Teresa?' he asked.

Richard took Mr. Craig's hand.

CHAPTER XVII

THE CLOSE

WOULD our mother have wished it?'
These words, uttered in a tone of grave,
sad questioning, were followed by a hush among
the group which sat under the trees in the orchard
that same afternoon. The two mares belonging
to Mr. Craig, and Juana's strawberry-roan, were
feeding close by, the summer flies their sole trouble.
The group consisted of Raphael Craig, the two
girls who, as he had said, were his daughters by
right of all he had done for them, and Richard.
Old Craig had, without any reservation, told Juana
and Teresa the history of their mother, and the
history of his vengeance on the man who had so
cruelly wronged their mother. He explained to
them, with a satisfaction which he took no trouble
to hide, how Simon Lock, after a career of splendour,
was now inevitably doomed to ruin. He told them
how for twenty years he had lived solely for the
achievement of that moment, and that, now it had
come, he was content.

But Juana had said, 'Would our mother have
wished it?' And her phrase reminded Richard
of the old man's phrase to Simon Lock in the

morning—'Hers was a gentle heart.' The sisters looked at each other, unquiet, irresolute.

'This Simon Lock is our real father, then?' said Teresa.

'Have I not just told you so?' said the old man.

'Let him off, father,' Juana murmured; and Teresa's eyes, though she said nothing, supported her sister.

'Why?' asked Raphael Craig.

'Surely you despise him too much to notice him. Is not the best punishment for him his own conscience and your silent contempt?'

'No,' cried the old man, suddenly starting up. 'No, I will never let him go free! After all these years of labour and sleepless watching, shall I take my hands off his throat now? You don't know what you ask, Juana. But you were always against me, Juana, ever since you were a little child—you who bear your mother's name, too!'

'Nay, father,' said Juana; 'I admire your defence of my mother. I love you for it. I think you are the noblest man alive. But you will be nobler if you let this man go free. He is beneath your notice.'

'Never!' repeated the old man, and walked quickly out of the orchard.

The three young people, left together, scarcely knew what to say to each other. The girls were, very naturally, excited and perturbed by the recital to which they had just listened. As for Richard, he was still in a state of suspense, of apprehension,

almost of fear. To him the very atmosphere of
Queen's Farm seemed to be charged with the
messages of fate. Raphael Craig's profound self-
satisfaction struck Richard as quite child-like.
Did this man, so experienced in the world, really
think that Simon Lock would quietly allow himself
to be ruined? Did he really think that the struggle
was over? And if, on the other hand, he thought
that Simon Lock would procure his arrest, was
he actually prepared to go to prison, and to die
there? Richard pictured Simon Lock as planning
all sorts of deep-laid schemes against Raphael Craig.
He felt that Simon Lock would never be 'at the
end of his tether,' as the old man had termed it,
until Simon Lock was dead. He felt just a little
bit for Simon Lock on account of the humiliations
which that proud personage had been made to suffer
that morning, and he felt so, despite his detestation
of Lock's past career and of his general methods.
He found it impossible to get very angry about a
sin committed twenty years ago.

That night Nolan, the detective, though better
than on the previous day, was suffering from a
slight temporary relapse. Richard volunteered to
sit up with him, as the man could only sleep at
intervals. Both Bridget and Juana were exhausted
with the nursing, and Juana would not hear of
Teresa sitting up. So it came about that Richard
insisted on performing the duty himself.

It was a warm summer night, rather too warm
for comfort, and for a little space the two men

talked on miscellaneous subjects. Then Nolan asked for something to drink, and having drunk, went off into a sound sleep. So far as Richard could see, the patient was better again. Richard occupied an easy-chair by the window. There was twilight all through the night. For a long time Richard gazed idly out of the window into the western arch of the sky. As hour after hour passed the temperature grew chilly. He closed the window. Nolan still slept peacefully. Richard drew down the blind, and said to himself that he would have a doze in the easy-chair.

The next thing of which he was conscious was a knocking at the door.

'Yes, yes,' he answered sleepily, and Mrs. Bridget burst in.

'Mr. Redgrave!' she cried, 'an' have ye heard nothing? Surely the ould master's not in his bed, and something's happened. May the Virgin protect us all this night!'

Richard saw wild terror in the woman's eyes. He sprang up. He was fully and acutely awake, but the sick man slept on. He went quietly and quickly out of the room. Juana and Teresa stood in the passage, alarmed and dishevelled.

'He is gone!' Teresa exclaimed. 'I wonder you heard nothing, as his was the next room. It was Bridget who heard a sort of shout, she says, outside, and then looked out of her window, and she thinks she heard a motor-car.'

'Which way was it going?' asked Richard.

'Sure and it's meself that can't tell ye, sir,' said Mrs. Bridget.

Richard reflected a moment.

'Why has he gone off like this in the night?' questioned Juana.

'Suppose that he has been captured—abducted —what then?' said Richard. 'Teresa,' he added, 'put your things on. You and I will go after him. Juana and Bridget must see to the nursing. Let there be no delay.'

His words were authoritative, and both girls departed. Richard proceeded to examine the bedroom of the vanished Raphael Craig. It was in a state of wild confusion. The bed had not been slept in; the bed was, indeed, almost the sole undisturbed article in the room. A writing bureau stood in the corner between the window and the fireplace, and apparently Mr. Craig had been sitting at this. The ink-bottle was overturned, the rows of small drawers had all been forced open, and papers, blown by the wind from the open window, were scattered round the room. The window was wide open from the bottom, and on the sill Richard noticed a minute streak of blood, quite wet. The wall-paper beneath the window was damaged, as though by feet. The window-curtains were torn. Richard judged that Raphael Craig must have been surprised while writing, gagged, and removed forcibly from the room by the window. He turned again within the room, but he observed nothing further of interest except that the drawers and cupboards of a large mahogany wardrobe had been forced, and their contents flung on the floor.

Richard went downstairs and out of the house by the front-door. He travelled round the house by the garden-path, till he came under the window of Raphael's bedroom, and there he found the soil trodden down and some flowers broken off their stalks; but there was no traces of footsteps on the hard gravelled path. He returned to the house.

'Mr. Craig has certainly been carried off,' he said to Teresa, who was just coming down the stairs, candle in hand.

She wore over her dress a coat, and a small hat was on her head.

'Carried off!' she exclaimed, and the candle shook. 'By whom?'

'Need we ask? Your father thought he had done with Simon Lock, but Simon Lock is not so easily done with.'

'But what can Simon Lock do with father?'

'Anything that a villain dares,' said Richard. 'Come along; don't wait. We will take one of the motor-cars and follow.'

They ran forth from the house to the sheds. The Décauville car stood in the first shed.

'Is it ready for action, do you know?' asked Richard.

'Perfectly. I had it out the day before yester-day.'

But when they came to start it they discovered that the pipe which led the petrol to the cylinder had been neatly severed. It was the simplest operation, but quite effective to disable the car. Nothing could be done without a new pipe.

'Where is the electric car?' Richard demanded almost gruffly. 'They may have missed that.'

'I don't know. It ought to be here,' Teresa replied.

'They have taken him off in his own car,' was Richard's comment. 'We can do nothing.'

'The horses,' said Teresa.

'No horses that were ever bred could overtake that car, or even keep up with it for a couple of miles.'

They walked back to the house, and met Bridget.

'Is it the illictric car ye're wanting?' she asked, with the intuition of an Irishwoman. 'It's in the far shed.'

With one accord Richard and Teresa ran back to the far end of the range of buildings. There stood the car, in what had once been the famous silver shed.

'I saw the master put it there this very morning as ever is,' said Mrs. Bridget, who had followed them, as Richard jumped on to the driving-seat.

In two minutes they were off, sped by the whispered blessings of Mrs. Bridget. At the end of the boreen Richard stopped the car.

'Which way?' he murmured, half to himself and half to Teresa, as if seeking inspiration. 'To London or to the North?'

'To London, of course,' said Teresa promptly. He hesitated.

'I wonder——' he said.

'What is that?' Teresa asked sharply, pointing to something which glinted on the road. She sprang down and picked it up. 'Father's spectacles,' she said—'cracked.' The spectacles had lain about a yard south of the boreen; they therefore pointed to London. 'Didn't I tell you?" said Teresa.

Richard shot the car forward in silence.

'Do you think dad threw out these specs. to guide us?' questioned Teresa.

'Perhaps,' answered Richard absently.

In this mysterious nocturnal disappearance of Raphael Craig he saw the hand of the real Simon Lock. During the whole of that strange interview which had taken place in the morning it had seemed to Richard that Simon Lock had been acting a part—had, at any rate, not conducted himself with that overbearing and arrogant masterfulness and unscrupulousness for which he had a reputation. Richard decided in his own mind that Simon Lock had arranged for his abduction, in case of necessity, before his visit to Raphael Craig. It was more than possible that he might have urged his visit chiefly as a visit of observation, to enable him to complete

his plans for exercising force to compel Raphael
Craig to agree to his wishes. With painful clear-
ness Richard now perceived that Simon Lock was,
in fact, fighting for all that he held most dear—
perhaps for his very life and liberty, in addition
to the whole of his fortune, for Richard knew that
when these colossal financiers do happen to topple
over into ruin the subsequent investigation of
their affairs often leads to criminal prosecution,
a process disagreeable to the financier, but
pleasant enough to the public. A man such as
Simon Lock had, therefore, a double, or, at least,
a highly intensified, motive in avoiding financial
failure. Yes, thought Richard, Simon Lock
would stop at nothing to compel Raphael Craig
to give way. His mind wandered curiously to
tales of the Spanish Inquisition, and to the great
torture scene in Balzac's 'Catherine de Medici.'
He involuntarily shuddered, and then with an
effort he drew his mind back again to the management of the car. This vehicle, new and in
beautiful order, and charged for a journey of a
hundred and twenty miles, travelled in the most
unexceptionable manner. The two and a half
miles to the North-Western station at Dunstable
were traversed in precisely five minutes, in spite
of the fact that the distance included a full mile
of climbing.

The electric lights flashed along the deserted
main streets of ancient Dunstable, which is only
a little more sleepy at night than in the daytime.

As they passed the Old Sugar-Loaf Inn a man jumped out of the stable archway and hailed them frantically. His voice echoed strangely in the wide thoroughfare.

'What is it?' demanded Richard, unwillingly drawing up.

'You after a motor-car?' the man inquired. He looked like an ostler.

'Yes,' said Richard.

'Mr. Craig?'

'Yes,' said Richard.

'They stopped here,' said the man, 'and they told me to tell you if you came by that they'd gone to Luton, and was a-going on to Hitchin.'

'They! Who?' asked Teresa.

'The gents in the car.'

'Who was in the car?'

'Four gents.'

'How long since?'

'About half an hour, or hardly.'

'And was it Mr. Craig who told you they'd gone to Luton and Hitchin?'

'How do I know his blooming name as told me?' exclaimed the man. 'They gave me a shilling to stop here and tell ye, and I've told ye, and so good-night.'

'Thanks,' said Richard, and he started the car. In another moment they were at the crossing of the two great Roman high-roads, Watling Street and the Icknield Way. The route to Luton and

Hitchin lay to the left; the route to London was straight ahead. Richard stopped again.

'Now, was that a fake of Lock's, or are we all wrong about Lock? and has your father got still another mystery up his sleeve?'

He gazed intently at the macadam, but the hard road showed no traces of wheels anywhere, not even their own.

'We will go straight ahead,' said Teresa earnestly.

Richard obeyed her instinct and his. Everything pointed to the probability that Simon Lock, anticipating pursuit, had laid a trap at the Old Sugar-Loaf to divert such pursuit. Then Raphael Craig must surely have been drugged, or he would have protested to the ostler.

Before they had got quite clear of the last houses of Dunstable they picked up Mr. Craig's gold watch, which lay battered in their track. If Craig had been drugged he must have quickly recovered! Teresa was now extremely excited, anxious, and nervous. Previously she had talked, but she fell into silence, and there was no sound save the monotonous, rather high-pitched drone of the motor-car. They passed through Markyate, four miles, and through Redbourne, another four miles, in quick succession. The road lies absolutely straight, and the gradients are few and easy.

'Surely,' said Teresa at length, 'if they are on this road we should soon overtake them at this speed?'

'Fifty miles an hour,' he said.

They were descending the last part of the hill half-way down which lies Redbourne. It was a terrible, perilous speed for night travelling, but happily the night was far from being quite dark. Though there was no moon, there were innumerable multitudes of stars, and the dusty road showed white and clear.

'Some cars can do up to seventy an hour. And if Simon Lock got a car he would be certain to get the best.'

As he spoke they both simultaneously descried a moving light at the bottom of the hill. In a few seconds the car was within a hundred yards of the light, and they could see the forms of men moving and hear voices.

'It is the other car broken down,' exclaimed Teresa. 'Put out our lights, quick!'

Richard realised in a flash that he ought to have taken that simple precaution before, and to have approached with every circumspection. The men in front had perceived the second car, and Richard's extinction of his lights came too late. He heard a sharp word of command, and then three men left the disabled car and ran in a body to the other one. Their forms were distinctly visible.

'Three to one!' Richard said softly. 'It looks like being a bit stiff.'

'No! Three to two,' Teresa corrected him. 'Here! Take this.' She handed him a revolver which she had carried under her coat. 'I just thought of it as I was leaving the house, and took it out of the clock in the drawing-room.'

His appreciation of her thoughtfulness was unspoken, but nevertheless sincere.

The three men were within fifty yards.

'Slip off behind and into the hedge,' he ordered. 'We shall do better from that shelter if there is to be a row.'

She obeyed, and they cowered under the hedge side by side.

'Get further away from me,' he said imperatively. 'You may be in danger just here.'

But she would not move.

'Whose car is this?'' cried a voice out of the gloom—a rough, bullying voice that Richard did not recognise.

'Never mind whose car it is!' Richard sang out. 'Keep away from it. That's my advice to you, whoever you are. I can see you perfectly well, and I will shoot the first man that advances another step.'

'Why?' returned the same voice. 'What's all this bluster for? We only want a bit of india-rubber for a ripped tyre.'

'It doesn't take three of you to fetch a bit of indiarubber. Let two of you get back, and then I'll talk to the third.'

'Get on, my lads,' another voice cried, and this time Richard knew the voice.

It was Simon Lock's; the financier was covered

with a long overcoat; he was the rearmost of the three.

Richard, without the least hesitation, aimed at Simon's legs and fired. He missed. At the same instant the middle figure of the three flung some object sharply towards the hedge in the direction whence the revolver-shot had proceeded, and Richard felt a smashing blow on the head, after which he felt nothing else whatever. He had vague visions, and then there was a blank, an absolute and complete blank.

The next thing of which he was conscious was a sense of moisture on his head. He opened his eyes and saw in the sky the earliest inkling of dawn. He also saw Teresa bending over him with a handkerchief.

'You are better,' she said to him softly. 'You'll soon be all right.'

Richard shook his head feebly, as he felt a lump over his eye. He had a dizzy sensation.

'Yes, you will,' Teresa insisted. 'It was very unfortunate, your being hit with that stone. You gave an awful groan, and those men thought you were dead; they certainly thought you were alone. I would have shot them, every one, but you dropped the revolver in the grass by this bit of a gutter here, and I couldn't find it till they'd gone. D'you know, they've gone off with our car? There was a man among them who seemed to understand it perfectly. I'm awfully glad now I didn't show myself, because I couldn't have done

anything, and I can do something now. Oh, Dick!
I saw them pull father out of their car—it's a big
Panhard—and put him into ours. He was all tied
with ropes. It will be a heavy load for that little
car, and they can't go so very fast. We must mend
their car, Dick, and go on as quickly as possible.'

'Can we mend it?' Richard asked, amazed at
this coolness, courage, and enterprise.

'Yes, of course. Look, you can see from here;
it's only a puncture.'

'But didn't one of them say they'd got no india-
rubber?'

Teresa laughed.

'You aren't yourself yet,' she said. 'You're
only a goose yet. That was only an excuse for
attacking us.'

Richard got up, and speedily discovered that
he could walk. They proceeded to the abandoned
car. It was a 40 h.-p. concern, fully equipped and
stored. The travellers by it had already begun
to mend their puncture when the pursuing car
surprised them. They had evidently judged it
easier to change cars than to finish the mending.
Speed was their sole object, and in the carrying
out of the schemes of a man like Simon Lock a
40 h.-p. Panhard left by the roadside was a trifle.
In twenty minutes the puncture was successfully
mended, both Richard and Teresa being experts
at the operation. The effect of the blow on Richard's
head had by this time quite passed away, save
for a bruise.

'And now for Manchester Square,' said Teresa, as they moved off.

'Why Manchester Square?' Richard asked.

'That is where they were going; I heard them talking.'

'It will be Simon Lock's house,' said Richard. 'I must go there alone.'

From Redbourne to London, with a clear road and a 40 h.-p. Panhard beneath you, is not a far cry. In a shade under the hour the motor-car was running down Edgware Road to the Marble Arch. Richard kept straight on to Adelphi Terrace, put up the car at a stable-yard close by without leave, and, having aroused his landlady, gave Teresa into her charge until breakfast-time. It was just turned four o'clock, and a beautiful morning.

'What are you going to do?' asked Teresa.

'I don't exactly know. I'll take a cab and the revolver to Manchester Square, and see what happens. You can rely upon me to take care of myself.'

He could see that she wished to accompany him, and without more words he vanished. In ten minutes, having discovered a cab, he was in the vast silence of Manchester Square. He stopped the cab at the corner, and walked to Simon Lock's house, whose number he knew. A policeman stood at the other side of the square, evidently curious as to the strange proceedings within the well-known residence of the financier. The double outer doors were slightly ajar. Richard walked

nonchalantly up the broad marble steps and pushed
these doors open and went in. A second pair of
doors, glazed, now fronted him. Behind these
stood a man in evening dress, but whether or not
he was a servant Richard could not determine.

'Open,' said Richard. The man seemed not to
hear him.

He lifted up the revolver. The man perceived
it, and opened the doors.

'Where is Mr. Lock?' Richard demanded in a
firm, cold voice. 'I am a detective. I don't want
you to come with me. Stay where you are. Simply
tell me where he is.'

The man hesitated.

'Quick,' said Richard, fingering the revolver.

'He was in the library, sir,' the man faltered.

'Anyone with him?'

'Yes, sir; some gentlemen.'

'How long have they been here?'

'Not long. They came unexpected, sir.'

'Well, see that you don't mix yourself up in
anything that may occur. Which is the library
door?'

The man pointed to a mahogany door at the
end of the long, lofty hall. Richard opened it,
and found himself, not in a library, but in a small
rectangular windowless apartment, clearly intended
for the reception of hats and coats. Suspecting a
ruse, he stepped quickly into the hall.

'Not that door, the next one,' said the man,
quietly enough. Richard followed the man's

instructions, and very silently opened the next
door. A large room disclosed itself, with a long
table down the centre of it. The place did not
bear much resemblance to a library. It was,
in fact, the breakfast-room, and the library lay
beyond it. At the furthest corner, opposite another door, a man was seated on a chair. His
eyes seemed to be glued on to the door which
he watched.

'Come along, Terrell,' this man whispered,
without moving his head, as Richard entered.

Richard accordingly came along, and was upon
the man in the chair before the latter had perceived
that another than Terrell—whoever Terrell might
be—had thrust himself into the plot.

'Silence!' said Richard; 'I am a detective.
Come out.'

The revolver and Richard's unflinching eye did
the rest. Richard led the astonished and unre-
sisting man into the hall, and then locked him up
in the hat and coat room, and put the key of the
door in his pocket. He returned to the other
room, locked its door on the inside, so as to pre-
clude the approach of the expected Terrell, and
took the empty chair in front of the far door. He
guessed that Simon Lock, and perhaps Raphael
Craig, were on the other side of that door.

'Up to now,' he reflected, 'it's been fairly simple.'

There was absolute silence. It was as though
the great house had hushed itself in anticipation of
a great climax.

Then Richard heard a voice in the room beyond. It was Simon Lock's voice. Richard instantly tried the door, turning the handle very softly and slowly. It was latched, but not locked. Using infinite precautions, he contrived to leave the door open about half an inch. Through this half-inch of space he peered into the library. He saw part of a large square desk and an armchair. In this armchair sat Raphael Craig, and Raphael Craig was tied firmly to the chair with ropes. He could not see Simon Lock, and he dared not yet push the door further open.

'Now, Craig,' the voice of Simon Lock was saying, 'don't drive me to extreme measures.'

For answer Raphael Craig closed his eyes, as if bored. His face had a disgusted, haughty expression.

'You've got no chance,' said Simon Lock. 'Redgrave is caught, and won't be let loose in a hurry. These two girls of yours are also in safe hands. Nothing has been omitted. I have here a list of the firms who have been acting for you in the Princesse shares. I have also written out certain instructions to them which you will sign. I have also prepared a power of attorney, authorising me to act in your name in the matter of these shares. You will sign these documents. I will have them sent to the City and put into operation this morning, and as soon as I have satisfied myself that all has been done that might be done you will be set free—perhaps in a couple of days.'

Richard saw that Raphael Craig made no sign of any sort.

Simon Lock continued: 'You did not expect that I should proceed to extreme measures of this kind. You thought that the law of England would be sufficient to protect you from physical compulsion. You thought I should never dare. How foolish of you! As if I should permit myself to be ruined by an old man with a bee in his bonnet; an old man whose desire is not to make money—I could have excused that—but to work a melodramatic revenge. If you want melodrama you shall have it, Craig, and more of it than you think for.'

'Why don't you give me up to the police?' said Raphael Craig, opening his eyes and yawning. 'You've got Featherstone's confession, as you call it. Surely that would be simpler than all this rigmarole.'

The manager's voice was pregnant with sarcasm.

'I will tell you,' said Lock frankly; 'there is no reason why I should not: I have lost the confounded thing, or it has been stolen.' He laughed harshly. 'However, that's no matter. I can dispense with that—now.'

'You can't do anything,' returned Craig. 'You've got me here—you and your gang between you. But you can't do anything. In three days your ruin will be complete.'

'Not do anything!' said Simon Lock; 'there are

ways and means of compulsion. There are worse
things than death, Craig. You decline to sign?'

Raphael closed his eyes again, coldly smiling.

'Terrell,' called Simon Lock sharply, 'bring
the——''

But what horrible, unmentionable things Terrell
was to bring in will never be known, for at that
instant Richard rushed madly into the room. He
saw a revolver lying on the desk in front of Simon
Lock. He frantically snatched it up, and stood
fronting Simon Lock.

'Well done, Redgrave!' said the old man.

Simon's face went like white paper.

'So "Redgrave is caught," is he?' said Richard
to Lock. Without taking his eye off the financier,
he stepped backwards and secured the door. 'Now,
Mr. Lock, we are together once more, we three.
Don't utter a word, but go and cut those ropes
from Mr. Craig's arms. Go, I say.' Richard had
a revolver in each hand. He put one down, and
took a penknife from his pocket. 'Stay; here is
a knife,' he added. 'Now cut.'

As Simon Lock moved to obey the revolver
followed his head at a distance of about three
inches. Never in his life had Richard been so
happy. In a minute Raphael Craig was free.

'Take his place,' Richard commanded.

In another two minutes Simon Lock was bound
as Raphael Craig had been.

'Come with me, dear old man. We will leave
him. Mr. Lock, your motor-car is in a stableyard

off Adelphi Street. You can have it in exchange for the car which you stole from me a few hours ago.'

He took Raphael Craig's arm, and the old man suffered himself to be led out like a child.

Within a quarter of an hour father and adopted daughter were in each other's arms at Adelphi Terrace. The drama was over.

. . . . .

Two days later the evening papers had a brilliantly successful afternoon, for their contents bore the legend: 'Suicide of Simon Lock.' It was a great event for London. Simon Lock's estate was found to be in an extremely involved condition, but it realised over a million pounds, which was just about a tenth of what the British public expected. The money, in the absence of a will, went to the heir-at-law, a cousin of the deceased, who was an army contractor, and already very rich. The name of this man and what he did with his million will be familiar to all readers. The heir-at-law never heard anything of the Princesse shares, for Raphael Craig, immediately on the death of his colossal enemy, destroyed the contracts, and made no claim whatever. This act cost him a hundred thousand pounds in loss of actual cash outlay, but he preferred to do it. Raphael Craig died peacefully six months later. Both the girls who had called him father were by that time married —Teresa to Richard and Juana to Nolan, the detective. It was indeed curious that, by the accident of fate, Raphael should have been saved from the consequences of the crime of uttering false coin by the spell exercised by those girls over two separate and distinct detectives. The two detectives—one professional, the other amateur—subsequently went into partnership, Nolan having retired from Scotland Yard. They practise their vocation under the name of——— But you will have guessed that name, since they are the most famous firm in their own line in England at the present day.

And Richard says to his wife: 'I should never have saved him. Everything might have been different if your courage had not kindled mine that morning after I swooned by the roadside in Watling Street.'

THE END

Books Published by
THE BOOK CASTLE

**NORTH CHILTERNS CAMERA, 1865–1939; FROM THE THURSTON
COLLECTION IN LUTON MUSEUM:** edited by Stephen Bunker
Rural landscapes, town views, studio pictures and unique royal portraits by the area's
leading early photographer.

JOURNEYS INTO BEDFORDSHIRE: Anthony Mackay
Foreword by The Marquess of Tavistock
A lavish book of over 150 evocative ink drawings.

**FOLK: CHARACTERS and EVENTS in the HISTORY OF BEDFORDSHIRE
and NORTHAMPTONSHIRE:** Vivienne Evans
Arranged by village/town, an anthology of stories about the counties' most intriguing
historical figures.

ECHOES: TALES and LEGENDS of BEDFORDSHIRE and HERTFORDSHIRE:
Vic Lea
Thirty, compulsively retold historical incidents.

TERESA of WATLING STREET: Arnold Bennett
Introduced by Simon Houfe.
The only detective story by one of the twentieth century's most famous novelists. Written
and set in Bedfordshire.

A LASTING IMPRESSION: Michael Dundrow
An East End boy's wartime experiences as an evacuee on a Chilterns farm at Totternhoe.

JOHN BUNYAN: HIS LIFE and TIMES: Vivienne Evans
Foreword by the Bishop of Bedford
Bedfordshire's most famous son set in his seventeenth century context.

LOCAL WALKS: SOUTH BEDFORDSHIRE and NORTH CHILTERNS:
Vaughan Basham
Twenty seven thematic circular walks.

DUNSTABLE IN DETAIL: Nigel Benson
A hundred of the town's buildings and features, past and present, plus town-trail map.

OLD DUNSTABLE: Bill Twaddle
A new edition of this collection of early photographs.

ROYAL HOUGHTON: Pat Lovering
Illustrated history of Houghton Regis from earliest times to the present day.

**OLD HOUGHTON, INCLUDING UPPER HOUGHTON, NOW PART OF
DUNSTABLE:** Pat Lovering
Over 170 photographs of Houghton Regis during the last 100 years.

Further titles are in preparation.

All the above are available via any bookshop,
or from the publisher and bookseller
THE BOOK CASTLE,
12 Church Street, Dunstable, Bedfordshire LU5 4RU. Tel (0582) 605670